HERO

HURRICANE RESCUE

HERO

HURRICANE RESCUE

JENNIFER LI SHOTZ

The #1 *New York Times* bestselling author

HARPER

An Imprint of HarperCollinsPublishers

This book is a work of fiction. Names, characters, places, and incidents are either the product of the author's imagination or are used fictitiously, and any resemblance to actual persons, living or dead, business establishments, events, or locales is entirely coincidental.

Hero: Hurricane Rescue
Copyright © 2017 by Alloy Entertainment

All rights reserved. Printed in the United States of America. No part of this book may be used or reproduced in any manner whatsoever without written permission except in the case of brief quotations embodied in critical articles and reviews. For information address HarperCollins Children's Books, a division of HarperCollins Publishers, 195 Broadway, New York, NY 10007.
www.harpercollinschildrens.com

Produced by Alloy Entertainment
1325 Avenue of the Americas
New York, NY 10019
www.alloyentertainment.com

Library of Congress Control Number: 2017934810
ISBN 978-0-06-256044-5 — ISBN 978-0-06-256043-8 (pbk.)

18 19 20   BRR   10 9 8 7 6 5 4 3

First Edition

For my kids, who are still patiently waiting for a dog. Soon, I promise!

1

HERO WAS PERFECT.

That was the only way Ben knew how to describe his dog.

Ben watched the black Labrador retriever's muscles flex as Hero vaulted into the air to catch a ball. Sunlight glinted off the dog's dark coat. His powerful legs stretched in either direction, as if they were carrying him on the wind. Hero's movements were fluid and precise.

Perfect.

Hero caught the ball in his powerful jaws and landed gently on the grass.

"Nice catch, Hero," Ben said.

"He never misses, does he?" Noah asked.

"Nope," Ben replied, pushing his brown curls out of his face.

Scout skidded over to Hero and tumbled to a stop between the bigger dog's front legs. The golden brown puppy with the white chest and paws looked up at Hero with huge, sad eyes and whimpered. Hero dropped the ball to the ground and nudged it toward Scout.

"Scout!" Jack laughed at his puppy. "You can't make Hero do all the work and then take the ball from him!"

"Well, he just did," Noah said, grinning.

"Hero will do anything for Scout," Ben said. "Right, Hero?"

Hero wagged his thick tail at the sound of his name. Ben gave him a scratch behind the ears.

Ben, Noah, and Jack spent nearly every day throwing the ball around in the baseball field near the woods. The boys were on their middle school's baseball team and had logged a lot of hours on this field, at practice and home games. This year, they'd had an amazing run—their team finished first in their division and almost made it to the state championships. The boys wanted to keep their skills sharp through the fall so they'd be ready for the season, come spring.

Ben took off his sweatshirt and threw it on the ground. It wasn't hot exactly, but it was humid, especially for this time of year. Ben had overheard his parents talking that morning about a big storm—something about a hurricane heading for Florida. That was a few hundred miles to the east of them. His dad had said Gulfport was going to be spared the worst of it but would still probably get walloped by rain and wind.

The dogs played on despite the oppressive weather. Scout loped off with the ball in his teeth. He snorted, swinging his black snout around in a goofy figure eight. Hero caught up to Scout in two long strides, ran past the puppy, then spun around to face him. Hero snatched the ball right out of Scout's mouth and bolted away.

"No way!" Ben cracked up. "Did you see that, guys?"

"Nice one, Hero!" Noah was laughing so hard he could barely speak.

"Hero's just reminding us who's in charge," Jack said. "I keep telling Scout to respect his elders, but he's not listening."

No one knew what kind of dog Scout was, but Ben could tell he was going to catch up to the large, muscular Hero one day—and then Hero would be in trouble. After Hero and Ben had saved baby Scout from a dogfighting ring, he'd gone to live with Jack at the beginning of the summer, after Jack's old dog passed away. Since then, the little mutt had almost doubled in size from a tiny puppy to about the size of a full-grown beagle. He was finally growing into his gigantic paws—but he still had a long way to go.

Because Scout and Hero wanted to play all the time, Jack and Ben had become really good friends, talking nonstop about their two favorite things: dogs and baseball. Ben played shortstop, and Jack was at first base.

That meant Jack and Noah—Ben's best friend since kindergarten, who was the team's starting pitcher—also hung out a lot. Ben wasn't always sure how much they liked each other, though. Sometimes he worried they just tolerated each other for his sake.

Hero zipped across the grass. Scout took off after him, his legs pumping hard.

"Look at that." Ben squinted into the early fall sunlight, watching the dogs go.

"What?" Jack followed his gaze.

"Scout's almost keeping up with Hero."

Hero sensed that Scout was closing in on him and picked up speed, leaving Scout in the dust.

"Well"—Ben shook his head—"almost. But Scout is definitely getting faster."

"And bigger too," Jack said. "He's taking up more room in my bed anyway."

Hero skidded to a stop. Scout was right behind him, but his reflexes weren't as quick. He smacked right into Hero, and the two dogs fell to the ground, playfully rolling around in the dirt. The ball fell out of Hero's mouth. Noah ran over and grabbed it, then held it out for the dogs to see.

Noah pulled his arm back and snapped the ball in a high arc. Hero and Scout took off after it. Noah ran after them.

"Go, Scout!" Ben shouted. "Get it, boy!"

"Aw, come on, Hero, don't let that little guy catch you!" Jack called out.

Ben thought he heard something off in Jack's voice. He watched as Jack stared far away across the clearing. He wasn't watching the dogs—he looked like he was thinking about something else entirely.

"Jack," Ben said. "Dude. You with us?"

Jack snapped his head around toward Ben.

"Sorry. I was just thinking . . ." He trailed off. He turned to watch the dogs lope back toward them, Hero gripping the ball tightly in his jaw.

"Is it about Scout?"

Jack shook his head.

"No. I just"—he looked up at Ben—"I was just thinking about my dad. I'm not supposed to see him for a few more weeks, but I really don't want to wait that long."

"That must be tough." Ben couldn't imagine not seeing his dad for weeks at a time. Jack's parents had gotten divorced almost a year earlier. He and his mom had come to live in Gulfport, but his dad still lived up north, in Jackson.

"I was thinking I might go see him sooner than that," Jack said. "Like, this weekend."

"That's great," Ben said. "Is your mom going to drive you up there?"

"Nope." Something in Jack's expression changed. "I'm going to go on my own. I'll call her when I get there and let her know where I am."

Ben wasn't sure what to say. How could Jack just leave town? And how was he planning to travel 150 miles on his own? A knot of worry rose in Ben's throat.

Noah trotted toward them with the dogs close on his heels.

"Jack," Ben said softly so Noah couldn't hear, "your mom will freak if you just take off like that. Have you even talked to them about it—your parents, I mean? Do they know how you feel? I bet your mom—"

"My mom won't understand," Jack cut him off.

"Okay, but—"

Noah ran up just then, out of breath but smiling. He tossed the ball to Jack.

"Hey," Noah said in between panting breaths. "Are you guys napping, or are you going to throw the ball again?"

"Definitely throwing the ball," Jack said, looking relieved to change the subject. "You go long again, Noah."

Noah groaned and ran back toward the other end of the clearing. Jack ambled toward Hero and Scout.

"Jack," Ben called after him. Jack turned to look at him. "You're not really going to try to get to Jackson on your own, are you?"

Jack shrugged but didn't say anything.

Ben tried to think of something—anything—to convince his friend not to go.

"You heard about the storm that's coming, right?" Ben asked.

Jack nodded. "You mean the storm that's heading for Florida? We live in Mississippi, remember?"

"Yeah, but my dad said we're going to get a lot of rain and stuff." Ben felt silly talking about the weather, but he was grasping at anything to get through to Jack. "It might get kind of nasty. If you're going to, like, take the bus or something, you don't want to get stuck in a storm on the road, do you?"

Jack shrugged again. "No, I don't."

"Soooo . . . does that mean you're not going to go?"

"If it really bothers you, I won't," Jack said, finally looking Ben in the eye. "And you're probably right. It's a terrible idea."

Ben wished he could believe his friend.

2

BEN STUMBLED DOWNSTAIRS FOR BREAKFAST THE next morning. Hero trailed along behind him and trotted over to his food bowl. Ben dumped kibble into it, more by feel than by sight, since his eyes were still blurry with sleep. He gave Hero the command to eat, and his dog began to chow down.

Ben yawned. He was exhausted—he'd tossed and turned all night worrying that Jack was going to try to get to Jackson on his own. Ben wanted to get to school a few minutes early to talk to Jack and be sure he wasn't really leaving town.

Ben's little sister, Erin, sat at the kitchen table with her backpack on and her tiny rolling suitcase parked right next to her. The TV was on in the background.

"Morning, Benny," she mumbled through a mouthful of waffle.

"Morning, Sis," Ben said, rubbing his face with his hands. "You and Mom aren't leaving for the airport for a while. Why do you have your backpack on already?" he asked.

"I don't want to miss my flight," Erin said matter-of-factly. Ben knew there was no point explaining the space-time continuum to a six-year-old, so he dropped it.

Ben's parents stepped into the kitchen mid-conversation.

"Do you think this storm is going to be bad?" his mom asked.

His dad turned his focus to the television. A meteorologist spoke in a serious voice.

". . . and that's the Gulfport weather. Meanwhile, the hurricane bearing down on our neighbors to the east is picking up strength. Communities on the southern tip of Florida are battening down the hatches right now. Experts say the storm is still on track to make landfall in Florida late tonight. This is going to be a bad one."

Ben's dad furrowed his brow and started tapping at

his phone. Ben recognized that worried look. It was a natural reflex for a police sergeant, and Ben had seen it on his dad's face a million times—but it still gave him an uneasy feeling.

"It sounds like it's too soon to tell," his dad said. "It looks like it's heading for Florida, which means we'll just get dumped on by the rain." He shook his head. "But you never know with these things. We've still got a few hours to go."

Ben's mom looked worried. His dad looked up from his phone and wrapped his arm around her shoulder. She rested her head against his chest for a moment.

"We'll be fine here," his dad said. "You should still go. We'll get you to the airport early, just in case."

"If you say so," she replied. Then her head popped up, and Ben could see that her brain was buzzing with last-minute reminders. Sure enough, she began to run through a list of things she'd already covered with them several times. "Don't forget Hero's appointment with the vet on Monday morning," his mom said. "It's at nine. He's getting his teeth cleaned. Oh, and you have to run by the pharmacy on Sunday. Remember they close early on Sundays. And then—"

"We got it," Ben's dad interrupted, smiling at her. "Just enjoy yourself. Don't worry—Ben and I have everything covered."

"Sure you do," his mom said with a laugh.

"Besides," his dad said, giving her a kiss on the cheek, "you're only going away for four days." He tilted his head toward Erin. "You should be more worried about how much your parents are going to spoil Erin while you're there."

"No kidding," Ben's mom groaned. "She'll be demanding ice cream morning, noon, and night—and they'll give it to her."

"Woo-hoo! Ice cream!" Erin fist-pumped.

Hero raised his head to look at Erin, then dropped his muzzle back into his breakfast. His metal tag jangled against his bowl.

"Please, Mom," Ben said, rolling his eyes in Erin's direction. "Don't bring her back any more of a pain than she already is."

Erin stuck her tongue out at Ben. Ben tousled her hair.

"I'm kidding, Sis." He grinned at her. "You're already the biggest pain possible."

Erin swatted at Ben, and he hopped up from the

12

table, just out of reach of her little hand.

"Very funny, Ben," his mom said, wrapping her arms around him in a giant hug. "You sure are getting tall, kiddo." She turned to his sister. "Erin, honey, we should leave now. I see you're all packed and ready."

"She's been ready since last week," Ben teased.

"Yeah," his mom shot back, "it's called being prepared. You should try it sometime."

Ben gave a fake laugh. "You're cute, Mom."

She smiled, then her expression turned serious.

"Seriously, Ben," his mom said softly while his dad carried Erin and her suitcase to the door. "Do me a favor and keep your dad out of trouble while I'm gone, would you? You've got Hero to look out for you, but if I'm not here, there's no one to look out for your dad. You know how hard it is for him to leave work."

Ben's dad was devoted to his job—that much was true. He cared about the people of Gulfport, and he'd been awarded all kinds of medals to show for it. Hero too. At the moment, Hero was just a dog on a mission to get the last crumb of breakfast in his bowl, but in fact, he was the most famous search-and-rescue dog in the history of Gulfport, Mississippi—maybe even all of Mississippi.

Back when Hero was his dad's K-9 search-and-rescue partner, Ben used to joke that Hero got to spend more time with his dad than Ben did. Now Hero was a full-fledged member of the Landry family—Ben had adopted him after he'd retired from the force a few months earlier—but Ben's dad still put in long hours on the job.

"I promise, Mom," Ben said, "we'll be fine. Noah's spending the weekend here too—remember, his parents are out of town?" His mom nodded. "We're just going to watch a lot of sports and eat a lot of pizza," Ben continued. "And I'll make sure Dad eats and leaves the house with pants on and all that stuff. That's what a good son does for his pops, right?"

The mention of a father and son brought back all of Ben's worry about Jack. A feeling of dread washed over him at the thought of Jack alone on the road, desperate to get to his own dad. Ben composed his face so that his parents couldn't tell there was anything wrong. His mom smiled at him as he walked her to the front door.

Hero trotted over to them and licked Erin on the cheek. She giggled and bent down to look Hero right in the eye.

"Hero, I'll see you Monday night, okay?" Hero licked her on the nose. Erin giggled again. "You can sleep in my bed if you miss me, okay?" Hero wagged his tail.

In a flurry of suitcases and boarding passes and stuffed animals, Ben's family drove off. Ben waved as they pulled out of the driveway. Hero leaned against Ben's leg and snuffled sharply through his nose.

"Let's go, pal," Ben said to Hero. "We gotta find Jack, and we'd better not be late for school."

3

"MAN, THAT ALGEBRA TEST WAS WAY harder than I thought it would be." Noah groaned on the way down the hall.

"No kidding," Ben replied. He ran over the equations in his head. There was still a chance he'd do well, but it wasn't going to be his best grade. He'd studied hard, but apparently not hard enough.

Ben looked around the crowded hall for Jack, but he didn't see him. He hadn't been able to find him earlier either. Ben tried to shake off the bad feeling as he and Noah slipped into their desks in English class.

"Listen up, everyone." Mr. Pang leaned over his desk, reading something on his laptop screen with a worried look on his face. The students stopped chattering, and the room went quiet. "It looks like there's going to be a change of plans today."

"Pop quiz?" a boy called out from the back, sending a wave of chuckles and groans across the room.

"I wish," Mr. Pang said. "But no. Everything is fine, but unfortunately it looks like the hurricane has started heading farther west, toward us." The students went silent. Ben exhaled slowly while he tried to wrap his brain around the news. "This just happened," Mr. Pang went on, "and there's still a good chance it won't make landfall and will just spin itself out over the Gulf. Either way, we're going to get soaked tonight. I'm going to need you all to remain very calm. School is dismissed early today—" The students broke out in a unified cheer, despite the news. "Quiet, everyone—please. Listen, your parents have been notified, and you are expected to leave the school now in an orderly fashion and head *directly* home. All after-school activities have been canceled, both at school and in town. Let's go, guys. Stay safe."

Ben and Noah scrambled to their feet and stuffed their books into their backpacks. They looked at each other.

"Uh, I guess I'm coming to your house early?" Noah said. His eyes were shaded with worry. "Great weekend for my parents to be out of town." High-fiving kids bumped and shoved past them, in a hurry to get out of school as quickly as possible.

"It'll be fine," Ben reassured him. "We've got Hero to keep us company. And maybe Scout and Jack will come over too. You haven't seen him today, by the way, have you?"

Noah rolled his eyes. "Scout and Jack this. Jack and Scout that," he said in pretend exasperation.

"Yeah, yeah," Ben said. "Very funny." He pulled his phone from his pocket and checked the screen. There were two texts from his dad. *Hurricane changed course. Could be bad for Gulfport,* his dad wrote. *Everyone needs to prep for storm & shelter ASAP. Coming to pick you & Noah up now.*

Ok thx, Ben wrote back. Then he texted Jack. *Totally not a good day 2 go see ur dad right?* he wrote. He waited. After a second, a return message popped up from Jack. It was two emojis: a winking smiley face, and a thumbs-up.

Ben had a weird feeling. It must have shown on his face, because Noah shot him a strange look.

"What's up?" Noah asked.

"Nothing," Ben said, wishing he sounded more sure of himself. "My dad's coming to get us. I have to get some stuff from my locker. Meet you out front in five?"

"Right. I'll be there," Noah said.

Ben pushed his way through the thick crowd of students jamming the hallways. He made a beeline for Jack's locker. Thankfully, Jack was there. Ben let out a sigh of relief. Jack closed the door and spun around to find Ben standing behind him.

"'Sup, Ben." Jack looked over Ben's shoulder, at the floor, even up at the ceiling—anywhere but at Ben. He shifted from one foot to the other.

"You're going to see your dad, aren't you?" Ben asked.

Jack didn't say anything. He opened his mouth as if to speak, but nothing came out. Ben took it as a yes.

"Jack. Seriously. Don't go," Ben said. "The storm is going to be bad. It's really not safe for you to travel right now."

"We don't even know if it's going to hit us." Jack hefted his backpack onto one shoulder. "They always exaggerate."

Ben racked his brain for something he could say to convince Jack not to get on the road by himself. "My dad just texted me from the station." He pulled

20

his phone from his pocket, as if that would be more convincing somehow. "He said we all need to take shelter—like, now."

"Well, how great that you have your dad here to look out for you."

"Come on," Ben said. "That's not what I mean. My dad's at work, and the cops have more information than we do. And he said—"

"Ben!" Jack cut him off. "Thanks, but I'm good."

"I'm sorry," Ben said, shaking his head, "but it's just not safe. . . ." Ben trailed off. He thought he saw something cross Jack's face—was it fear? For a split second, Ben was hopeful that he'd gotten through to him, but then the faraway look returned to Jack's face.

"I know you're just trying to help." Jack looked up and locked his eyes on Ben. "But *if* I did go see my dad, you wouldn't tell anyone, right?"

Ben studied Jack. He was torn—he knew it was a bad idea for Jack to go. But he also knew that if the roles were reversed, Jack would keep Ben's secret. That's what friends did. Right?

"Fine," Ben finally said. "I wouldn't tell anyone."

Jack held up his closed fist. Ben bumped it.

"You better get home, man. Hero's waiting, right?"

Jack started to walk away. The crowd of students was thinning as the school emptied out.

Ben started to walk away too, then spun back around and called after Jack. "What about Scout?" Jack was totally devoted to the puppy. Surely he would never put the dog in danger? "I can't stop you from going, but you can bring Scout to my house, okay?"

Jack stopped and turned to look at Ben. He shook his head.

"Thanks. But I never said I was going."

"Right," Ben said softly to himself as he watched Jack walk away. "You never said you were going. Got it."

4

BEN'S HEAD WAS SPINNING.

He couldn't believe Jack was acting like this. He knew Jack wasn't quite himself because he really missed his dad. But was he really going to hit the road—with Scout—during a massive storm?

Ben just wished his friend had given him a straight answer. He'd promised Jack he wouldn't tell anyone about his plan, and Ben couldn't go back on his word. If Jack wasn't really leaving but Ben broke his promise—well, then Ben would just look like a bad friend and everyone would be upset for nothing.

He stood alone in the hallway. The school was

practically empty—all the other students had taken off as quickly as possible.

Ben tried to think logically, but the thoughts just ran circles in his head. Just as he felt like his brain was about to implode, his phone buzzed in his pocket. *Phew,* Ben thought. *Jack's calling to say he's been messing with me.* He fished it out and answered without even glancing at the screen.

"Dude—" Ben started.

"Ben? It's Dad. I'm out front. Where are you?"

"Oh, uh—hey, Dad. I'm still inside. Sorry, I'm coming now."

"Noah's already with me. Hurry it up, Ben. I need to get back to work."

"Okay—coming." Ben clicked off the call and scrambled down the hall to his locker. He spun the combination lock as quickly as he could, grunting as books tumbled out of the locker and into his chest. He caught them before they hit the ground. Ben slammed his locker shut and raced outside.

The gray sky hung low over the school.

Ben ran to his dad's police cruiser idling at the curb. He hopped in, and with one look at his dad's face he knew that the storm was going to be really bad. Noah sat in the back, his face white as a ghost and his eyes rounded with worry. Ben's stomach dropped.

"Ben, this isn't public information yet," his dad started, his voice low and serious. "We just heard this about ten minutes ago." He steered the car out of the parking lot. "No one expected this, but the hurricane hasn't just headed farther west. It's moving north, too—toward land. It's totally changed course, and it's headed right for Gulfport, son."

"Are you serious?" A chill went through Ben's body.

"Yeah. Dead serious." His dad pressed his lips together.

"Are Mom and Erin okay? And Noah's parents?"

"Their flights took off before the airport got too backed up. They all landed safely. Everyone's fine and out of the path of the storm."

Ben exhaled.

"When? I mean, when will it hit?"

"We still have a few hours."

Ben took a moment to absorb what his dad was saying. "So what now?"

"Now we make sure we keep people safe. It's all hands on deck at the station, and it's going to be a long night."

Ben understood what that meant. His dad would be

at work until the storm had passed and he knew the people of Gulfport were okay. And he and Noah would need to look out for themselves.

"Here's the thing, boys," his dad went on. "The governor is scrambling the National Guard and lots of backup right now, and her people need a few more minutes to get everything in place before she announces it on the news. Once she does, people are going to start panicking. There isn't enough time to evacuate, so we're going to have to get people to shelter in place. It's not going to be easy."

Ben shuddered at the thought of all the people in his town feeling terrified and freaking out. He pictured them all calling the police station at once. And his dad would be the one to help them. Pride surged in his chest—but was quickly replaced with worry for his dad. He wished they could all be at home together. But that's not what happens when your dad is a cop.

"So I'm going to get you back to our house," his dad was saying, "and I need you to stay there."

"Yeah, of course." Ben turned to look at his pale, scared friend in the backseat. "Don't worry," Ben reassured him. "It's going to be fine, okay?" Noah nodded.

"Noah, I promised your parents I'd keep you safe,"

Ben's dad said. "I need to know that you boys are in the house and out of harm's way, okay? If I know *you're* safe, I can help other people—you get that, right?"

"We get it, Dad."

"Yes, Sergeant Landry."

Ben studied the sky. It was a solid mass of clouds and rain. He looked for the horizon but couldn't make it out. Everything had turned the same flat, suffocating gray. *Which direction would the hurricane come from?* he wondered.

He felt his dad looking at him.

"Ben?"

"Yeah?"

"I'm counting on you—you understand that?"

"Of course, Dad."

"No heroics with Hero, right?"

"No heroics with Hero, Dad. Promise."

"Okay." They drove in silence for a few blocks. "You guys will need to do a few things around the house for me."

"Sure," Ben and Noah said in unison.

"I know what to do, Dad," Ben said. No hurricanes had hit the town in Ben's lifetime, but he'd seen his parents prepare for some near misses in the past. They had also reviewed emergency steps in school a million times. "We'll board up the windows—"

"Boards are in the basement," his dad interjected.

"—and we'll put all the outdoor furniture and garbage cans into the garage."

"And Mom's potted plants."

"Yep, Mom's potted plants. And we'll have to go do the same things at Noah's house, right?"

"Right," Noah said from the back.

"Okay, but then you have to go right back home," his dad said, looking at Noah in the rearview mirror. "Once the storm starts, I want you both to take Hero and get into our basement. Stay there until either I tell you it's okay to come out or you hear the siren from town telling you the storm is over. You understand? Don't come upstairs for anything."

"We won't."

"Charge your phones. Make sure the flashlights are within reach. Turn off the gas . . ."

Ben nodded as his dad ran down the list.

"Tell me again," his dad finished. "You're not going to leave the house once the storm starts, right?"

Ben's dad wasn't the kind of parent who repeated things. He didn't usually need to. As a police sergeant,

he was used to people doing what he told them to do—
and Ben rarely disobeyed. Well, except for once or twice
when Hero and Scout were missing. Oh, and when he'd
led Noah into the middle of a dangerous gang of dogfighting criminals. But that was different. Ben couldn't
just sit still when someone he loved was in danger. But
who would go out in a hurricane?

One terrifying thought occurred to Ben: *Jack*.

Would Jack be crazy enough to try to get to his dad's
house with a hurricane barreling down on them? Would
he try to get out of town before the storm hit?

Ben broke out in a cold sweat. He put his hand on
the phone in his pocket, ready to call Jack. He wanted to
call or text his friend right away, but he didn't want his
dad to know anything about Jack's plans. He'd promised
he'd keep his mouth shut.

There was no way Jack would go now, Ben told
himself.

He would never take the risk. Especially not with
Scout.

Would he?

"And don't forget Hero's food . . . Ben? You listening
to me?"

"Yes—sorry, Dad."

Ben tried to pay attention, but his mind was on his friend. Jack was sad and angry about his family—Ben got that. But that didn't make it okay for Jack to take Scout and head out, alone and unprepared, into a storm that could threaten their lives.

5

BEN AND NOAH WERE IN OVERDRIVE. They stood outside and banged nails through boards into the window frames.

They went back inside and raced around the house, carrying supplies downstairs to the basement and running back up for more. Ben gave Hero a few things that he could carry in his strong jaw. Hero seemed to understand that these were important tasks.

Ben and Noah took a can opener, dozens of cans of food, and bags of kibble to the basement. They set up air mattresses and carried blankets and sheets down too. Ben found the crank radio that they could use to get updates and emergency instructions. He charged his phone and Noah's.

And every few minutes, he checked his phone screen to see if Jack had texted or called. As soon as Ben's dad had pulled away from the house—after an extra-tight hug—Ben had gone into the bathroom where Noah couldn't hear him and called Jack. There was no answer. He'd left a message. "Please," Ben had begged his friend, "just tell me you're okay and you're not going. This is really serious."

No response.

When they were done at Ben's house, the boys hopped on their bikes and rode as quickly as they could to Noah's, Hero chasing alongside them. Hero scurried into Noah's backyard and started nosing at all the things they needed to move.

"Thanks, Hero." Noah chuckled drily. "Don't worry—we'll take care of all the heavy lifting."

"Today is one of the rare days when I wish you had thumbs, Hero." Ben groaned as he tried to lift a massive wrought-iron deck chair. Hero wagged his tail at the sound of his name. "Just kidding, buddy." Ben finally gave up and started dragging the chair toward the garage. Hero ran ahead of him, leading the way.

Ben checked his phone. It was four o'clock, but it felt much later. The sky had darkened to a steely gray and the air was heavy. It pressed down on him from above. Ben could feel the barometric pressure dropping—the storm was getting closer. The thick, still air had a sound-dampening effect, but Ben could hear Noah's neighbors on both sides hammering boards over their windows.

They finished, and Noah shut and locked the door behind them. "Let's go," he said. "I just want to lie down on an air mattress in your basement and go to sleep. Wake me when the hurricane is over."

"No kidding," Ben said. His whole body was exhausted. But he barely noticed—he was too distracted by the fact that he still hadn't heard from Jack.

The boys pedaled as fast as their tired legs could go, Hero trotting along with them. They reached the corner. If they turned left, they'd head straight for Ben's house. If they turned right, they would be going toward Jack's house.

They stopped to check for oncoming cars. In that second, Ben made a decision. Noah started to turn left. Ben turned right. Hero ran alongside Ben's bike.

"Dude!" Noah called out, slamming on his brakes. "Where are you going?"

"Gotta swing by Jack's house. You go on ahead. I'll meet you at my house in a minute."

Noah looked anxious. He glanced up at the sky, then back at Ben. The worst part of the storm wasn't supposed to hit for a few more hours, but there was no telling how much longer they had before the advance front of rain and wind kicked in.

"We really need to get to your house. The storm is going to be here soon."

"It's okay, it'll just take a few minutes."

"Why do you need to go to Jack's? Can't you just call him?"

"Uh, he's . . ." Ben scrambled to think of an answer. He didn't want to lie to Noah, but he also couldn't break his promise to Jack. "I just want to make sure Scout is okay. I'm sure he's scared by all the activity and the weather. It'll make him feel better to see Hero." It wasn't technically a lie. It was just part of the truth.

Noah groaned. He pedaled in a circle and rode up next to Ben.

"Fine," Noah said. "I'm coming with you."

They rode toward Jack's house. Ben felt terrible for

keeping the truth from his lifelong best friend, but he didn't know what else to do. He needed to talk to Jack in person and try to convince him—again—not to do anything stupid.

Thunder rumbled in the distance. They had to hurry.

Jack's house was dark and quiet. Ben rang the bell, a prickly feeling running up and down the back of his neck. A long silence followed. He was about to ring again when he heard footsteps. Finally, the door swung open, and Jack's mom stood in the doorway, a look of surprise on her face.

"Oh, hello, Ben," she said. She wore her white doctor's coat and was tapping out a text into the phone in her hand, even as she gave Ben a distracted look. Ben could hear the television in the background. A newscaster was instructing viewers to shelter in place. "Sorry, I was out back putting some things away." She looked down at Hero, who stood by Ben's legs. "Hi, Hero."

Hero sniffed at the air just inside the house, looking for Scout.

"Hi, Dr. Murphy. I was just . . ." Ben trailed off. Something told him to stop talking. Jack's mom was looking over his shoulder, a half smile painted on her lips.

"Where's Jack?" she asked. "And Scout?"

Ben quickly processed the meaning of her words. She thought Jack and Scout were with him.

Because Jack must have told her they were with Ben.

Because Jack and Scout weren't here.

A bolt of fear shot through Ben. He tried to fight off the rising sense of panic. Maybe there was another explanation. But right now he needed to get back home so he could think about what to do next.

"Oh, they're back at my house," he said as casually as he could. He hoped his face didn't betray how uncomfortable he felt about lying. "Noah and I"— Ben gestured over his shoulder at Noah, who gave a quick wave from the sidewalk—"had to run over to Noah's house to get a few things, but Jack stayed at my place." Ben's brain was running a thousand miles a minute, trying to come up with a remotely plausible explanation for why he was there. "And I promised him I'd swing by here and pick up some extra puppy food for Scout."

She looked at Ben with a curious expression, as if she were deciding whether or not to believe him. But then she smiled and said, "Oh, of course, honey.

Come on in. I'll just get it for you."

"Great, thanks." Ben stepped into the front hall-way of Jack's house. Coats, sweatshirts, and dog leashes dangled from hooks in the entryway. Chew toys and tennis balls littered the floor. Ben stood there awk-wardly, trying not to count the number of lies he'd just told. *They weren't real lies*, he told himself. *They were just to buy time.*

"I'm so grateful to you for letting Jack come to your house during this awful storm," Jack's mom said. "I feel terrible that I can't be home with him, but I have to get back to the hospital. All doctors are required to report for duty until . . . Well, we'll see how bad it gets and what we find after the hurricane passes."

"Oh, it's no problem, Dr. Murphy," Ben said.

"Anyway," she said with a distracted smile, "I know Jack and Scout will be safe with you and Hero. Please tell your parents I said thank you. I'm sure your dad is having a busy day too."

"Yes, ma'am, he is."

"Be right back." Jack's mom disappeared around a corner, headed toward the kitchen. With a furtive glance in her direction to make sure she wasn't look-ing, Ben reached up and grabbed Jack's baseball team

37

sweatshirt off a hook. He stuffed it into his backpack.

He thought it might come in handy as a scent item, just in case his worst fears were confirmed. In case Jack was trying to get to his dad's house with Scout.

But Ben really hoped he wouldn't need it.

6

THE RAIN HADN'T STARTED YET, BUT the wind was picking up. Tree limbs bent and bobbed at sharp angles. Entire tree trunks swayed from side to side.

Ben's eyes burned from the grit and dirt that flew into his face. He and Noah rode through the nearly empty streets of Gulfport, pedaling hard against the wind. Even Hero looked like he had to work just to move forward, his eyes squeezed almost shut and his ears pressed back against the sides of his head.

"What the heck was that about?" Noah shouted over the noise of the gusting, whistling wind.

Ben knew he couldn't keep the truth from Noah any longer. Plus he didn't want to. His chest was tight with worry about Jack and Scout—and with stress from being the only one to know Jack's plan. Keeping secrets was a miserable job.

"It's Jack," Ben shouted back. "His mom doesn't know this, but he took Scout and left town."

"Left town?" Noah cried, pulling up beside Ben so they could hear each other better. "Now?! Where is he going?"

"To see his dad. In Jackson."

Noah shook his head.

"That's the worst idea I've ever heard," Noah called out.

"I know, and I need to find him fast. I don't even know if he's heard that the hurricane is headed straight for us. And I'm afraid he and Scout are going to get stuck in it. He's not answering his phone."

"So what are you going to do?" Noah asked.

"Hero and I are going to find him."

Until he said the words out loud, Ben hadn't been entirely sure what his plan was. But now he was certain of what he needed to do.

The boys didn't speak for a few blocks. The neighborhood was empty except for a couple of stray cars quickly heading to their final destinations. The wind continued its dance down the abandoned streets. Screen doors slapped shut, then flew open again. Ben felt the moist air thickening all around him, like it was wrapping him in a heavy, wet blanket.

Ben tried to focus and map out the steps in his head. He knew Jack would have to head north on the main road, Route 49, to get out of town. But that only led to more questions. How long ago did Jack leave? Maybe he'd tried to take the bus, but Ben was pretty sure that a bus wouldn't run in this weather. Was he on foot or on his bike? How far ahead were he and Scout? The road led right through the woods outside of town. Was it safer in the forest during a hurricane—or more dangerous? Could Ben and Hero even catch up to Jack now if they tried?

A huge *crack* shot through the air, and a blur of movement flashed before Ben's eyes.

"Whoa!" Noah screamed, pulling his bike sharply to the side and skidding to a stop. Ben slammed on his brakes just a couple of inches from him.

A massive tree branch had fallen across the road. It stretched from one side of the street to the other.

Ben pictured Jack and Scout in the woods, surrounded by tall, strong trees bending and sending branches toppling in the wind—just like this one. He couldn't imagine how terrified and alone they would feel when the storm really hit.

Fat raindrops began to pelt Ben on the face. He touched his hand to his cheek, where the water had stung his skin. More drops struck him on the head. The rain was starting—and already it was intense, forceful.

"Let's get out of here," Noah called out. He steered his bike up onto the sidewalk and across someone's lawn to get around the tree. Ben and Hero followed closely behind.

The rain picked up speed. The boys reached Ben's driveway just as the skies opened and a curtain of rain came down. They stashed their bikes in the garage and ran inside, water running off them onto the kitchen floor. Ben grabbed a stack of towels. He tossed one to Noah, then dropped to his knees and held a towel out toward a soaking Hero. But Hero didn't want to dry off. He walked away from Ben to the front door and stood by it, waiting. He watched Ben carefully, and Ben knew exactly what his dog wanted.

Hero wanted to go get Jack and Scout. He knew they were in trouble.

"Okay, buddy." Ben sighed and looked at Noah. "I

guess Hero and I are heading back out now. The full hurricane's not supposed to hit for a couple more hours. You'll be safe here. We'll be back soon."

Noah tossed his towel onto the back of a chair. "I'm coming with you."

Ben shook his head. "That's not a good idea."

"Is it a worse idea than going alone to Jackson in a hurricane?"

"I don't want anyone else to be in danger."

"Well, it isn't all up to you, Ben. I don't want you to be in danger either. Especially not by yourself."

Ben thought about what his friend was saying. He realized that Noah wanted to help him the same way Ben wanted to help Jack. And there was no way Ben would take no for an answer if the roles were reversed.

"Okay," Ben exhaled. "Thanks." He tried to shake the feeling that not one but now two of his friends would be in danger. Ben and Hero would have to bring their A game—more than ever before. "We need some supplies," Ben told Noah. "Rain gear, water, food, a radio."

"Got it," Noah said. "I'll start packing up." He grabbed his backpack and started making room in it. "How do you think Scout will do in a storm?" Noah asked.

At the mention of Scout's name, Hero let out a soft bark. He whimpered and paced by the front door. He was anxious to go.

"Hero, buddy, sit," Ben said from across the room. Hero sat but didn't look happy about it. He followed Ben with his eyes. The dog's whole body was jittery and tense.

Ben filled water bottles and stuffed them into his backpack. He dug around in the mudroom for rain ponchos and his dad's spare rain pants and waders. He snatched up a handful of protein and granola bars, trail mix, and lots of treats for Hero. His backpack weighed about a zillion pounds by the time he was done, but he knew he might need everything in it. Every few minutes, he stopped to call Jack. It went straight to voice mail. Jack was ignoring his calls.

Noah stood by the door in Ben's mom's rain gear—a coral-colored slicker and pants—with a scowl on his face.

"Sorry, dude," Ben said. "That's all I could find."

"It's fine," Noah said. "Let's just get going."

Hero was up on his feet, his tail wagging, his eyes pleading with Ben to hurry.

Ben ran upstairs to get something from his dad's

closet. He came back down, his arms full of gear for Hero. Without any commands from Ben, Hero sat down and waited expectantly for Ben to suit him up.

Ben slipped a stiff neon yellow rain vest over Hero's head. It circled his neck and extended along his back to his tail. The front flap covered his chest and reached under to his belly. The sides hung down low. Ben buckled the nylon straps under Hero's chest and stomach, holding the vest in place. There were reflective strips along the top and sides so Hero could be seen in the dark.

"Looking good, Hero," Noah said.

Hero gazed up at Ben, ready to go. Finding people was what Hero was trained to do—what he had done on the police force for years, for as long as Ben could remember. And he did it better than any other dog out there.

"I know, pal," Ben said, rubbing the top of Hero's head. "I want to go find them too." He had stuffed Jack's sweatshirt at the top of his backpack. He pulled it out and held it under Hero's nose. Hero ran his snout over the fabric, sniffing and exhaling sharply, sniffing again, then snorting again. He did this dozens of times before sitting down and looking at Ben, waiting for a command.

Ben studied Hero's face, with its shiny dark fur and

expressive eyes. Hero couldn't speak, but Ben felt like they always understood each other anyway. Hero had Jack's scent. He was ready.

"Let's go," Ben said.

With a last look around his warm, safe, and dry house, Ben turned the doorknob. As soon as it was unlatched, the door flew open, pushed hard by the howling wind outside. The door knocked Ben in the chest. He stumbled backward, almost tripping over Hero. Horizontal rain flew into the house.

"The storm is getting closer!" Noah shouted. "We need to hurry!"

Ben grabbed hold of Hero's collar and, with the other hand, pointed in a *go* command toward the door. Noah led the way, bending forward and tipping his head down, keeping his face out of the intense wind and rain. They pushed ahead and made it to their bikes.

All the houses were locked up tight. Everyone in the neighborhood had shut their doors, boarded their windows, and retreated to safety inside.

Ben had never pedaled so hard in his life. The boys could barely move in a straight line—they slalomed all over the road, just trying to keep biking forward. Rain lashed at their faces. Ben shook his head to get the water out of his eyes so he could see where they were going.

All he had to do, really, was follow Hero. It was clear to Ben that even in the rain, with the wind blowing so hard, Hero had latched on to a scent. Hero barreled forward through the darkening, soaked streets, his yellow vest flashing. Water flooded the gutters, and trees bent in the heavy wind.

Ben and Noah followed Hero as closely as they could. Hero made a few turns and led them north, toward the edge of town. Ben kept expecting Hero to head for the smooth pavement of Route 49, but he stuck to smaller roads. Where was Hero taking them? Would Jack and Scout really have traveled along this winding route?

But then, after a couple of miles, Ben realized why Hero wasn't taking them to the road.

Because his dog was leading them straight into the dark, wet woods.

7

THEY REACHED THE EDGE OF THE forest, and whatever light was left in the sky was soon obliterated by trees. Ben and Noah followed Hero just inside the tree line. They stopped to catch their breath. The rain beat down, and the trees sounded like a raging sea, crashing back and forth above them.

Ben wiped the rain off his face and shook out his hands. His fingers were pruny and stiff from gripping the wet handlebars for so long. Tree branches snapped overhead. Branches plummeted down, some catching on lower limbs, others crashing to the ground.

"Maybe we should turn back," Ben said, loudly enough to be heard over the wind and rain. "This is getting really dangerous." Before Noah had a chance to reply, Hero barked several times at Ben. He was agitated—he pranced in a circle, then ran a few feet farther into the woods, then stopped, turned back to Ben, and barked again.

Noah surveyed the darkness ahead. He looked at Ben. Just as Noah opened his mouth to speak, Hero barked, then shot off deeper into the forest. He disappeared from their sight within seconds.

"Hero!" Ben called out. "Stop!" But it was too late. Hero was long gone. Ben turned to Noah. "I'm sorry—I can't leave Hero out here by himself."

"Me neither," Noah said. "Let's go."

The boys pedaled off after Hero. Once they were farther inside the protective enclosure of the thick foliage, the wind and rain weren't as bad. Ben used a flashlight to light the way. The narrow beam bounced off the trees closest to them, leaving everything beyond them in utter darkness. He saw a tiny dot of flashing, reflective yellow bouncing in the distance—Hero's vest.

They wove around trees, following the path Hero had taken, which was muddy and thick with leaves and debris. Their fat bike tires barely turned in the muck. Ben's legs ached, and his lungs burned.

Ben wasn't familiar with the spot where they had entered the national park—it wasn't anywhere near where the boys practiced baseball, or where he and Hero had been the day they'd found Scout.

After a few minutes of hard riding, Ben saw Hero stop up ahead to sniff at something. Ben tried to pedal faster on the muddy ground so they could catch up, but his front tire struck something hard and fixed—a root or a big rock. He managed to hang on to the handlebars and catch himself before he went flying over the front. Noah slid to a stop behind him.

"We need to ditch the bikes," Ben said, hopping off and letting his bike fall to the ground. He would worry about finding it again later.

"Yeah." Noah dropped his bike to the ground too.

The boys moved ahead on foot as quickly as possible. Hero's ears twitched as he watched Ben and Noah get closer. The sky was barely visible through the tops of the trees that loomed over them—trees as tall as buildings.

Ben turned off his flashlight and followed the reflective strips on Hero's vest. He couldn't even make out Hero's dark fur. Ben heard Noah right behind him.

They traveled for a mile or more, deeper into the

woods—and the farther they went, the more Ben felt they should stop. They should turn around and go back to the safety of his house. They should dry off and hunker down and pray that Jack and Scout would be okay.

This was a terrible idea.

Suddenly Hero stopped, and Ben and Noah came to a halt too. Hero raised his head and looked around. His ears pricked up, and he sniffed at the wind. Then, with a yelp, he quickly sat down and turned to look at Ben, his eyes full of urgency.

This is what Hero was trained to do when he found what he was looking for.

But there was nothing there—just trees, and rain, and darkness. Ben's heart sank. Had Hero's tracking skills been thrown off by the storm?

Ben was about to ask Hero what he had found, when he suddenly heard a small, familiar bark not too far off in the woods.

Scout!

"Go, Hero!" Ben called out, giving Hero the hand signal to go along with the command. "Go get Scout!"

Hero dashed toward the sound of Scout's bark. Tripping over vines and roots, Ben and Noah followed the dog as closely as they could. Hero stopped short, and Ben and Noah paused. Scout's high-pitched barking was much louder and closer. The puppy had to be nearby—right?

So why had Hero stopped? And why wasn't Scout running to them?

Before Ben had a chance to find out the answers, the hair on the back of his neck stood up. His skin tingled. It was like an electrical current passed through the air all around him. He looked up and realized that the world had gone silent. The rain above them had stopped. The wind had ceased. The trees were still, and everything was frozen. It was as if someone had pushed the *off* button on the weather.

Ben knew that was what happened right before things got bad. They were in the eye of the storm.

About ten feet away, he spotted a small cove created by two downed trees leaning against a low hill. The space was just big enough for the three of them to squeeze into—and just big enough to protect them.

"There!" Ben shouted, pointing with one hand and grabbing Noah's slicker with the other. They dashed toward the shelter, with Hero herding them along. The two boys and Hero tucked themselves into the small space and huddled together.

They ducked their heads, wrapped their arms around each other's shoulders, and held on tightly.

The hurricane was about to hit.

8

BEN WAS TREMBLING, AND HE COULD feel Noah shaking too. The tall trees waved back and forth. Ben hoped their trunks and branches would be able to withstand the worst of the wind. If they got knocked over, they'd land right on Ben, Noah, and Hero, trapping them—or worse.

And if that happened, Ben's parents would probably never find him. They would never know how sorry he was for coming out here.

But it was too late to turn back. Too late to run and hide in the dry safety of his basement. They were stuck here now, and they were about to ride out the worst storm in Ben's lifetime.

Ben buried his fingers in Hero's fur, which radiated warmth, and felt his dog's steady breathing. *Breathe*, Ben heard his dad's voice say. That's what he always told Ben to do first if he was in a bad situation. *Breathe. Stay focused. Find a solution.*

Ben inhaled and exhaled in time with the rise and fall of Hero's rib cage, trying to calm his own nerves. The smells of wet earth, wood sap, and crushed leaves filled his nose. Slowly, Ben's heart rate began to come down and he could think a little more clearly.

The seconds dragged by as the air crackled. It felt like forever, until finally it happened: A blast of air and a deluge of water slammed into them, hard, knocking them sideways. Ben clutched Hero for dear life as the storm washed over them. The wind was so strong it sounded like shrieking. Ben thought it would rip off his rain gear. The downed trees over their heads protected them from above, but the wind and rain were coming at them from every other direction. The pelting drops felt like a thousand tiny knives scratching at his face.

"Hang on!" he shouted at Noah over the din.

"Trying!" Noah yelled back, his voice filled with fear.

Hero's body was coiled and tense under Ben's hands as the boys huddled over him. "It's okay, Hero," Ben whispered into Hero's ear. "I got you, boy. I'm right here. We're going to be okay."

The sound of the rain and wind became a steady white noise in Ben's mind. He shut his eyes and tried to think of it like music. Every few minutes, he heard the sharp crack of a tree branch snapping in the woods around them—followed by the heavy thud of it hitting the ground.

Ben, Noah, and Hero were lucky. No branches landed on top of them.

But what about Jack and Scout? Ben opened his eyes and looked out into the storm. A wall of water beat down right outside their small, covered space. Ben peered through it and saw massive trees leaning left and right like they were blades of grass. Leaves and dirt flew by sideways.

Ben could only hope that Jack and Scout had been able to find a safe place to hide from the worst of the storm.

Finally, just when Ben's ears had started to ring from the din of the storm, the lashing wind and rain began to die down.

It seemed like the worst of it had passed—at least for now.

Ben and Noah crawled out from under their shelter and slowly stood up. Hero squeezed out between them.

The boys took in the forest around them. Ben almost couldn't believe his eyes: The thickly wooded forest looked like it had been turned upside down. The ground was carpeted with wet leaves and broken branches. But the trees were still standing.

"We must have been on the outer edge of the storm," Noah said, shaking his head in disbelief.

"We got lucky." Ben tugged at a giant leaf that had adhered itself to the side of his head. It came off his face with a slurping sound. "But it seemed like it was moving that way," Ben said, pointing back the way they came. "That has to mean . . ." He couldn't force himself to say the rest out loud.

"It's about to hit town," Noah finished for him. The boys were quiet for a moment, considering what that could mean. Ben pictured the streets of his quiet neighborhood flooded with water, houses with the roofs torn off—in his mind it was a darkened, empty wasteland. And what about his dad? Ben could hardly bear to think about where he was at that moment. Was he helping someone else find shelter—and had he gotten caught in the worst of it?

He wanted desperately to get back to town. He wanted to find his dad and make sure he was okay. He wanted to see if their house was still standing. But he couldn't do any of those things while Jack and Scout were still lost in the forest. He needed to finish what he had started. They were close to Scout, which meant they were close to Jack.

They couldn't stop now.

Hero seemed just as upset as Ben felt. He was staring through the rain at a spot deeper in the woods. He whimpered and paced back and forth, then stopped and stared again. Ben had never seen his dog this agitated. Hero barked a few times, then waited.

It made Ben shudder to picture Scout—who wasn't even fully grown yet, who was still just a sweet young dog—out in these woods getting batted around by this powerful wind and rain. Could he possibly have survived?

Hero barked again. There was silence for a second.

In the distance, they heard a sharp, quick bark. It was faint but clear.

"That's Scout!" Ben shouted.

Hero raced toward the sound of Scout's voice. Ben and Noah followed close behind. Scout's bark was growing louder, and Ben expected the puppy to run to them any second. He had to be so close—but where was he?

Hero froze. His ears shot up, and he stared at something a few feet ahead. Ben fished his flashlight out of the pocket of his slicker and pointed it about ten feet ahead of him: There was Scout, in the center of a clearing, jumping up and down excitedly and barking. Suddenly it was clear why he hadn't run to them. Scout was trapped on a tiny island, surrounded by rushing water.

And Jack was nowhere to be seen.

Hero barked at Scout. Scout responded with a few short, frantic yelps.

"Scout!" Ben called out across the water. "Come here, boy! Swim to us."

Ben knew Scout was a good swimmer. He and Jack had taken the dogs to the river a few times, and the pup was a natural. He'd jumped right in with Hero and spent hours on end paddling around in wide circles, lifting his snout just above the water line to breathe.

But Scout wouldn't go in the water this time. Ben watched, puzzled, as Scout took a few steps toward the small lake before him, lowered his nose, put one paw in the water, then immediately pulled back.

Hero started to wade into the water on their side. But Ben stopped him. "Hero, stay," Ben commanded him.

Something didn't feel right.

"What is it?" Noah asked.

"I don't know." Ben shook his head. "But there must be a reason Scout won't go in. Maybe it's too deep . . ." He trailed off, studying the land and water in front of them. He walked a few yards in each direction. The island wasn't big—it was twenty feet wide at most.

"How did Scout get there in the first place?" Noah asked.

"I think the water rose around him," Ben said. "That wasn't an island before this storm hit."

"And if Scout's here," Noah said, "where's Jack?"

"Good question."

Hero ran back and forth along the edge of the water, looking for a way to get across.

"We're going to get him, Hero. Just let me think." Ben turned to look for a long tree branch, or something else they could use to make a small bridge.

Hero barked, but his tone had changed. His yelps

grew more urgent and turned into a growl. He bared his teeth, his ears moving back on his head.

"What is it?" Ben asked, alarmed.

He waved his flashlight across the surface of the water, trying to see what Hero saw. At first there was nothing—until two gleaming red spots popped up in the darkness, then disappeared, almost as if they were never there.

Ben knew what those spots were. Growing up in Mississippi, he'd been trained from an early age to look out for them whenever he was near water at night. There were swamps and rivers everywhere in these woods. And those red eyes were unmistakable.

It was an alligator.

"Oh, man," Noah groaned.

"Hero—stay!" Ben commanded more firmly than ever before. Hero froze. Ben's heart pounded in his chest. The water rippled just under the surface. The alligator's greenish black skin blended in with the color of the water.

Ben could just make out the hard bumps on its back and tail. It was a big one, at least nine feet long. As he watched, the alligator raised its lumpy, mottled head back out of the water and opened its gaping jaw, revealing a long row of sharp teeth. Ben shuddered.

He had no doubt the giant reptile would snap up Hero or Scout if they tried to cross.

"Hero, come!" Ben said. Hero trotted over to his side, his eyes still on the underwater creature. Scout whimpered sadly on the other side. He dashed back and forth, crying for help.

"Scout, sit!" Ben commanded. Scout sat but kept barking. His whole body shook, and he rocked anxiously back and forth from one paw to the other.

"That thing must have been in one of the swamps nearby," Noah said. "And the flooding pushed it here. What are we going to do?" He spoke softly, as if he was afraid the alligator could understand him.

"I'm not sure," Ben replied. He squinted at the far side of the island, behind Scout. "I guess we could go around to the other side and try to cross there. We'll just have to hope there aren't more alligators. And that we can get to Scout before this guy"—he gestured at the alligator—"gets a whiff of us."

Noah nodded. "Let's go." He started off to the left. Ben trudged after him, his boots making a deep sucking sound with each step through the muddy terrain.

"Come on, Hero," Ben said. He heard Hero's collar

jingling behind him. "Good boy," Ben said. Hero kept close to his side. Ben heard his dog's breath in the quiet night.

They made their way along the water, but kept a safe distance from it. Alligators were quick, and Ben didn't want to be within snapping range. Every few feet, he looked back to see if the alligator had followed them. It hadn't. Scout ran along with them on his island, keeping pace with them.

Suddenly, Ben felt Hero brush against his leg. There was a rush of air as Hero took off like a shot, heading straight into the water.

"No!" Ben and Noah both cried. But Hero couldn't be stopped. He took one long leap and landed lightly in the water, about halfway across the creek. Ben was terrified. He looked back at the alligator. It had disappeared.

The water was deep. Hero swam hard, holding his nose and mouth high and kicking fast with all four legs.

"Hero!" Ben yelled. "Hurry! Go!"

"Faster, Hero!" Noah cried.

Ben saw ripples in the water close to Hero.

"Go, go, go!" Ben shouted. He almost couldn't bear to watch. Ben was about to turn away when Hero put one front paw, then the other, on land. He pulled himself out of the water and onto Scout's island just as the alligator raised its head above the surface right behind him. Hero snatched up Scout by the scruff of his neck and, holding the puppy in his jaw, ran as far away from the giant reptile as possible.

The alligator lowered itself into the water.

Ben let out a choked cry that was part relief, part fear. Hero was amazing—he'd made it to Scout. But now he—and Scout—had to get back. He looked up to see Hero staring intently at him. Hero put Scout down gently, as far from the alligator as he could. Ben held Hero's gaze, trying to understand what his dog wanted to tell him.

Then Hero did something Ben wasn't expecting: He dashed back toward the alligator in the water.

"Hero, no!" Ben yelled.

9

HERO STOPPED, BUT ALMOST AS THE words were out of Ben's mouth, he realized what the dog was doing: Hero was going to distract the alligator so Scout could get to safety.

That gave Ben an idea.

"Hold this," Ben said to Noah, handing over his soaking wet backpack.

Ben took a few steps toward the water and nodded at Hero. "Go!" he commanded his dog.

Hero ran toward the water's edge, barking aggressively. Just as the alligator raised its head out of the lake, Ben got a running start and jumped into the surprisingly cold water. The water was higher than his waist, and the bottom was silty and slippery under his feet. Branches, tree bark, and other debris crowded the surface and knocked into Ben. He stumbled and waded across as fast as he could—pulled back by the drag of his heavy rain gear.

Ben focused on reaching Scout. He tuned out everything else, just like he did when he was trying to catch a hard line drive from home plate.

He heard Hero barking off to his left. Out of the corner of his eye, he saw a quick flash of movement. The alligator's front half was on land. His giant jaw stretched open, revealing his sharp, angled teeth again. Hero snarled and barked ferociously. All the fur on his back stood on end. He splayed out his front legs and lowered his neck and head into a fighting stance—nothing was going to stop Hero from saving Scout.

Ben's stomach flipped as the alligator snapped his jaw shut with a loud *clack*. Hero barked and ran a few feet away, then zigzagged back across the beach. He moved toward the creature, then pulled away. The alligator's head swiveled side to side, confused. Hero was toying with the massive reptile, buying Ben time.

Ben plunged through the cold water. He felt the ground slope upward and fell to his knees as he reached dry land. Scout leaped toward him. Ben held out his arms, and Scout jumped into them. The puppy was big now—Ben could barely wrap his arms around him. Scout's body trembled with fear. He buried his head in Ben's neck. Ben felt the dog's hot breath in his hair.

"It's okay, Scout. I got you."

Ben held Scout tightly and cast a quick glance toward Hero and the alligator. The alligator scooted farther forward onto land, its tiny legs scuttling across the ground. Hero held his ground. His top lip curled up, and he bared his teeth.

Ben needed to hurry. He turned and stepped back into the rushing water. It felt even colder than before.

"You got this," Noah yelled encouragingly.

The water filled the pockets of his slicker and weighed him down. Ben had to pause each time he put a foot down to make sure he had good traction—all while gripping Scout tightly and keeping one eye on the alligator and Hero.

Suddenly, the alligator shot toward Hero and snapped its jaw. Hero jumped out of the way just in time.

Ben knew Hero wouldn't stop playing this horrible

but brave game with the alligator until he and Scout were safe.

Ben slipped on a rock but caught his balance before he fell. He squeezed Scout so tightly he could feel the puppy's ribs between his hands—he wasn't going to risk letting go.

Rain was dripping down Ben's face, blocking his vision, but he didn't wipe it away for fear he'd lose his balance. "I can't see," Ben yelled out to Noah.

"You're halfway across," Noah called out. "Keep going straight ahead."

Ben moved toward Noah's blurry shape, following the sound of his voice as much as anything else.

"Good," Noah said. "Like five more feet. You got it."

Finally, Ben felt the ground even out under him and the water receding. He released a sigh of relief.

"You can let Scout go," Noah said.

Ben loosened his hold on the puppy, who jumped out of his arms. Noah bent down and scooped up Scout. Ben dragged himself up onto land, catching his breath and wiping the water out of his eyes.

"Nice work," Noah said to Ben. Scout wriggled in Noah's grasp and let out a happy bark.

At the sound of Scout's voice, Hero's head shot up. He took off along the mud at top speed, accelerating from a standstill to lightning fast. The alligator followed, chasing him across the island.

But on land, at least, Hero was faster. In the blink of an eye, he was twenty feet away from the alligator, hurling himself into the water. His front paws popped up through the surface as he paddled furiously toward Ben.

Hero was more than halfway across the river when the alligator slithered back into the water, where it could move a lot faster than a dog could swim. The alligator disappeared under the surface. Ben couldn't see it, but he knew it was heading straight for Hero.

Ben knelt down on the bank. "Faster, Hero! Come on, boy! Swim faster!"

Hero's nose was just above the water, his mouth closed, as he pumped his legs and pushed forward.

"Let's go, Hero!" Noah yelled as Scout barked in his arms.

"Come on!" Ben screamed. "Let's go, let's go!"

Just as Hero put his front paws on the ground near Ben, Ben saw the alligator skimming the surface of the water right behind him. Hero vaulted himself onto land, and the alligator opened its massive jaw, snapping it shut on air. Hero shook off the water, sending a spray of moisture in every direction.

Hero, Ben, Noah, and Scout jumped backward.

"Let's get out of here!" Noah yelled. Still holding Scout tightly, Noah took off into the woods, the way they had come.

Ben snatched up his backpack from the ground. "Hero, come!" They ran after Noah. As they stepped back into the thick tree line from the clearing, Ben turned to look over his shoulder. The alligator had followed them up onto land. Now it eyed them coolly for a second, then waddled back into the water, disappeared beneath the surface, and swam away.

The boys stopped to catch their breath. Noah high-fived Ben.

"That was close," Ben said, feeling queasy. He dropped to his knees, wrapped his arms around Hero's neck, and held him tight. They were both soaking wet. "That's my boy."

Scout sauntered over and positioned himself right under Hero's chest. Ben scooped him up in the hug. Hero sniffed at the top of Scout's head and stuck his nose under Scout's chin. Scout slid out of Ben's grasp and dropped onto his stomach in the wet dirt. He rolled onto his side. The terrified and shaking puppy began to relax. Scout felt safe again with Hero there to protect him.

Ben fumbled around in his backpack for some dry clothes, glad that he'd thrown an extra pair of pants and a shirt in there at the last second. His hands were so cold he could barely feel anything, but he changed quickly, then shook out his rain gear and put it back on.

Drier and a little bit warmer, Ben exhaled. Scout and Hero were safe. But his joy at beating the alligator and saving the puppy faded quickly as an urgent question surfaced in his mind.

Where was Jack?

10

THE RAIN WAS HOLDING AT A steady downpour, and the wind was still strong.

"Scout," Ben said, "where's Jack?"

Hero's and Scout's ears pricked up at the sound of Jack's name. Ben tugged Jack's sweatshirt from his backpack. He held it under Hero's, then Scout's, noses. They took turns inhaling and exhaling it.

Hero moved away from Ben and sniffed at the ground. He stepped carefully around the area, his nose investigating the underbrush and scattered storm debris. Hero's ears rose, first rotating forward, then swiveling backward. His fur rippled as his muscles tensed and flexed, ready to spring into action.

"Let's go, Hero," Ben said, picking up his backpack. But Hero didn't move. He was looking at Scout—waiting for him.

Scout was sniffing hard at the ground too. He followed a scent, stepping lightly across the wet ground. Suddenly his head popped up, and he stared off into the distance, his floppy ears rising. Then Scout shot off farther into the woods, and for a frightening second, Ben thought he had bolted in fear. But Hero didn't seem concerned, so Ben took a cue from his dog. Hero stayed put, watching the spot where Scout had disappeared, waiting.

Scout suddenly reappeared between two trees. He barked twice, turned around, and took a few steps. He looked over his shoulder and barked again, as if telling them to hurry up. Hero trotted toward Scout and stopped. The dogs were waiting for Ben and Noah.

"Ben, we need to hurry," Noah said, his voice strained. "We need to get back before people realize we're missing."

His friend was right. They'd been gone for hours, and they had to be at least two miles into the woods by now.

But they were so close to finding Jack—which is why they had risked coming out here in the first place. There was no stopping now. Ben knew it, and Noah did too.

With a resigned sigh, Noah started walking.

The boys trailed after the dogs. They were back under the thick canopy of trees, so the rain and wind weren't too bad. But it was dark, and Ben's flashlight only lit up the area a few feet ahead of them.

Hero moved silently through the thick underbrush, the reflective strips on his vest floating smoothly through the darkness. Scout tripped and stumbled on every vine and branch. Yet the smaller dog forged ahead, determined in his mission to lead them to Jack.

The boys worked hard to keep up with the dogs, but it was a lot easier to move through the storm debris if you were on four legs and had incredibly sharp vision, a nose for danger, and killer reflexes. Ben and Noah were stuck with two feet and stiff rain gear, hauling mud-filled boots and heavy backpacks.

Ben reached for his phone and opened up his GPS app. Service was spotty, and the map wasn't much help this far out in the woods anyway. It just showed green mountains and no trails. Thankfully he didn't have a message from his dad yet. He must be pretty busy in town—and, Ben thought with some guilty relief, he probably assumed that Ben and Noah were safe and dry at home.

"I guess we better do this the old-fashioned way," Ben said. He pulled out a compass from his backpack and held it out in front of him. He shined his flashlight on it.

"I feel like we're on some survival TV show," Noah quipped. "But at least we're not in our underwear."

Ben laughed. Despite the circumstances, his spirits lifted slightly.

They were continuing northeast, away from Gulfport. He needed to keep track of where they were going so he could get them back home later.

They couldn't walk side by side in the dense forest. Noah marched a few feet ahead, and Ben brought up the rear. Suddenly Ben heard a thump, and Noah let out a loud grunt.

"You okay?" Ben called out.

"Yeah, I just tripped," Noah replied over his shoulder. He slowed down for a second so Ben could catch up to him. "You okay?"

"Oh, great," Ben said with a little laugh. "I mean, my best friend, my dog, and I just survived a hurricane but now we're lost in the woods looking for my other best friend—oh, and we just saved his dog, who was trapped on an island across alligator-infested waters. It's, like, a perfect day."

"Well, when you put it that way . . ." Noah joked. It was quiet for a moment as they started walking again. "Actually, though . . ." Noah's voice grew serious. "Can I ask you something about that 'other best friend'?"

Ben had a feeling where this conversation was headed. There was no way anyone would ever replace Noah in his life, and Noah had been cool with Ben hanging out with Jack so much. But still . . . Ben sometimes felt like things had changed between him and Noah, in a way that was hard for him to put his finger on. But Noah had never mentioned it, and Ben didn't know how to ask him.

Ben felt a little twinge of guilt. "What about him?" he asked.

"Nothing, really," Noah said.

Ben could tell that wasn't true. "Doesn't sound like nothing," he prodded gently.

"Well, I guess—I mean, I'm just . . ." Noah trailed off. "When did he get so important to you?" he continued. "You know—important enough to come out here and find him?"

It was a fair question. Ben thought about it. They had only met Jack a few months earlier, but Noah and Ben had been friends for almost a decade. In some ways, though, time had nothing to do with it. It was more like a gut feeling—sort of like how Ben felt the day he and Hero met Scout. He just knew Scout belonged in his life.

That's how Ben felt about Jack—even though Jack *had* been kind of a jerk at first. He'd been cocky and competitive with Ben, and rude to Noah. But after Ben had gotten to know him a little better, he'd realized that Jack just wasn't sure *how* to act. He was the new kid in town, and he really missed his dad and his old life and his old friends. Until he'd moved to Gulfport, Jack had lived his entire life in the same place. He'd never had to make new friends before—which was good, because it turned out he was really lousy at it.

That didn't make Jack a bad person, though—just a lonely one.

Noah had never really gotten past that first impression of Jack. Ben had been hoping it would happen over time.

"I don't know," Ben started. "I mean, I know he can seem kind of . . . tough or mean or something." He struggled to put into words why he thought Jack wasn't such a bad guy. "It's like Jack was alone for a while until we started hanging out, you know? And his family kind of sucks right now. But he's a good guy, I swear."

"Yeah, I know," Noah said. "Jack's cool. It's just that you wouldn't be out here in this"—he held his hands palms up in the air, gesturing at the sky and trees above them—"for just anyone. Neither would I."

"You didn't have to come—" Ben started to say.

"That's not what I mean," Noah cut him off. "I know I didn't. But was I supposed to let you come out here by yourself?"

Noah's words felt like a punch in Ben's gut. He'd been so worried about Jack and Scout that he hadn't stopped to think about Noah. Noah was just doing for Ben what Ben was doing for Jack.

"Thanks," Ben said. "For coming out here with me, I mean. It's a lot less scary with you here."

"You're welcome," Noah said.

"And I know Jack gives you a lot of grief," Ben said. "But I really think you'd like him if you got to know him better. Can you just give him a chance?"

Noah sighed. "Okay. But first we have to find him."

11

SCOUT'S HIGH-PITCHED BARK CUT THROUGH THE darkness ahead of them. Hero caught up with him and they let out a chorus of barks.

"Come on!" Noah said. He took off running. Ben followed as quickly as he could. He stumbled, trying hard not to trip in the darkness. Water drops flew into his eyes.

"Jack!" Noah cried out from a few feet ahead.

"What is it? Did you find him?" Ben skirted a pile of branches and wet leaves and stopped short. The two dogs had stopped next to a downed tree. Scout was jumping up and down excitedly, his tail wagging a mile a minute. Hero sat quietly, his front paws perfectly together, and looked at Ben, waiting for his command. Noah was on his hands and knees, inspecting something on the ground. He turned back to Ben with a worried expression on his face. "Did you find Jack?" Ben repeated.

Noah nodded.

Ben ran over and couldn't believe his eyes: Jack's legs were jutting out from under the long trunk of the fallen tree. His body was on the other side. He wasn't moving.

"Jack!" Ben shouted, panic rising in his chest. "Are you okay? Can you hear me?"

There was no response.

"Jack!" Noah and Ben called out.

Jack stirred.

"I'm okay," came his weak voice from the other side of the trunk. He sounded like he had just woken up. At the sound of Jack's voice, Scout went crazy. He whimpered and yipped. "Hey, Scout," Jack said.

Ben let out a burst of breath and smiled. A look of relief washed over Noah's face. Ben's chest tightened, his emotions a physical sensation.

"I can't get up," Jack croaked. Scout began digging at the ground by Jack's legs, trying to get his owner out.

Noah looked up at Ben, his eyebrows raised. *This isn't good*, he mouthed at Ben. Ben shook his head.

"Jack, man, can you feel your legs?" Ben's voice broke on the words. He braced himself for Jack's answer. There was a long pause.

"Yeah. I can feel them. I'm wiggling my toes."

Ben looked at Jack's boots. They were moving. "That's great!" Ben said.

"Yes!" Noah pumped a fist in the air.

"Okay," Ben said to Jack. "Give us a minute while we figure out how to get this thing off you."

Noah pointed to one end of the tree. "Check this out," he said to Ben.

Ben followed Noah's hand and saw that the top of the trunk was resting on a pile of debris. The pile had absorbed most of the weight when the trunk fell—saving Jack's legs from serious injury.

"Wow," Ben said. "You were seriously lucky, man."

"Really? This is 'lucky'?" Jack shot back. Ben was glad to hear a note of sarcasm in his friend's voice. That meant he wasn't too bad off.

"The tree landed on some other stuff, so it's not all on you."

"Well, it kind of feels like it's all on me, so why don't you wimps lift this thing off me already?" Jack cracked.

85

"You know we can still leave you here, right?" Ben groaned.

"Yeah, Jack, sorry—I need to get home for dinner," Noah chimed in. "But we'll come back tomorrow."

"Very funny, you two." Jack paused. "For real, though," he said, his voice getting quiet. "What are you guys doing here? Did you come out here to find me?"

"We can talk about that on the way home," Ben said. "I'm just—I mean, I'm really glad you're okay."

A booming crack of thunder shook the air around them. All five of them—human and canine—jumped at the sound of it. "We need to hurry," Ben said softly to Noah. "Sounds like the storm is picking up again."

"Can you lift it off?" Jack asked from the other side, a hint of desperation in his voice.

Ben wrapped one arm around the trunk and tried to shift the weight of it a little. He couldn't—it was too heavy. Jack grunted as Ben handled the tree. Even though the full weight wasn't on Jack's legs, it still had to be pretty uncomfortable.

Ben stepped over the tree trunk, careful not to bump it. Jack was lying back against a tree branch. He gave Ben a weak smile and a thumbs-up.

"Sit tight, okay?" Ben said to his friend.

"Like I have a choice."

"Good point." Ben crouched down to inspect the tree where it made contact with Jack's shins. Hero leaped over the trunk and landed lightly next to Ben. Scout barked from the other side.

"Hey, Hero," Jack said. Hero sniffed at Jack's legs. Ben shone his flashlight along the underside of the tree trunk.

"I guess you were right, huh?" Jack said to Ben. "This was a really stupid idea."

"Like I said, we can talk about that later." Ben grinned at his friend. "But yeah. It was. Now stop talking for a minute. I'm trying to think."

Another clap of thunder cracked overhead. Jack looked up at the sky. A worried look crossed his face.

"It's okay," Ben said to him. "We'll get you out of here, Jack."

Jack looked back at Ben with tears in his eyes. "Thanks, Ben."

"You got it."

"Okay," Noah called from the other side. "Can we try to lift this thing?"

"Yeah. On three," Ben replied. "You count."

"One," Noah began. He and Ben squatted down on

either side of the tree and put their hands under the trunk. "Two. Three."

The boys strained to lift the trunk off Jack's leg. It didn't budge.

"Man," Ben said with a grunt, "it doesn't look *that* heavy."

"Trust me," Jack said, "it's heavy."

Ben stepped back to survey the situation. A brilliant burst of lightning lit up the sky for a second, then everything went black again. A few seconds later, a deep rumble of thunder vibrated around them. Ben took a few steadying breaths. The worst of the storm was over, he told himself. If anything, they'd just get more wet. They could handle that.

"We could push from the same side," Ben said to Noah, "but then it would either have to roll over his legs or onto his chest."

Noah shook his head. "That wouldn't be good."

"Nope," Ben concurred. He snuck a look at Jack's face. Jack had his eyes closed. His nostrils flared as he took short, quick breaths.

Ben's brain was churning with ideas, but all of them ended with Jack getting hurt. Then it hit him: They didn't need to move the entire trunk off his leg.

They just needed to lift it enough so that Jack could pull himself out from under it. "Okay," Ben said, hopping to his feet and brushing his hands together to get the dirt off. "I got it."

Luckily he had thought to throw a long nylon leash of Hero's in his backpack. He worked quickly, looping it twice around the tree. Next, Ben found a large rock nearby. With a lot of grunting, he and Noah rolled it through the mud. They nudged it into position, up against the fallen tree. They would use it as leverage to brace the tree trunk as Hero pulled from the leash.

"Okay," Ben said, double-checking that everything was in place. "Now I just need you, Hero." Hero trotted over to him. Ben snapped the hook of the leash to the loop on the back of Hero's vest. Ben locked eyes with Jack. "You ready, man?"

"I'm ready."

"You know what you need to do?"

Jack nodded. "As soon as the pressure lets up, back up as quickly as I can."

"And get out of the way," Ben said.

"And get out of the way," Jack repeated.

"Your arms still work, right, Jack?" Noah joked.

Jack pushed himself up on his elbows. "Looks like it."

"Noah, you ready?" Ben asked.

"Yep." Noah was positioned across from Jack, lying in the mud on his back. "I'll lift from this side." He exhaled slowly.

Ben nodded. He squatted next to Hero and put a hand on his dog's head. "You just need to pull the tree trunk as hard as you can, okay? I'm right here to help you." Hero nudged Ben's face with his wet nose.

Ben wrapped his arms around the trunk.

"On three. One. Two. Three—Hero, go!"

Hero tried to run forward, but the weight of the tree snapped him to a full stop. He dug his paws into the wet dirt and strained hard against the harness. As Ben struggled to help lift the tree, he checked the setup, making sure nothing could hurt Hero or Jack. He eyed the harness—so far it was holding. No signs of tearing yet. Noah was flat in the mud, pushing the trunk from underneath. Ben could tell that the trunk had moved a little. But it wasn't enough.

"Come on, guys, we got this!" Ben called out through gritted teeth. "You okay, Jack?"

"I'm good," Jack grunted. Ben could tell the shifting weight of the trunk was causing him some pain. Scout let out an anxious bark and skittered around them. "It's okay, Scout," Jack said.

As Ben strained against the tree, he felt a fat raindrop hit his cheek. Then another. Then it started to pour.

Water slicked down Ben's face, mixing with sweat. Slowly, inch by inch, the trunk shifted onto the large rock. This was it. They just needed to raise it a centimeter—not even half an inch. "Go, Hero!" Ben cried. "Come on, Noah!" And with that, Hero pulled harder, Ben lifted, and Noah pushed so hard that his face turned bright red. Finally, the leash stretched tautly over the top of the rock, and the tree trunk rose up and off of Jack's legs.

"Jack—can you move?" Ben yelled.

"Almost!" Jack cried. He sat up and used his fingers to dig at the mud around his legs. Scout pawed frantically at the earth on the other side of the tree.

"Hurry!" Noah said through gritted teeth. "I can't do this much longer."

Jack planted his hands in the mud and started to scoot himself backward. Ben looked at Hero. The dog's head was stretched forward, his ears back flat on his head, and his eyes were focused on a spot in the distance. His tongue hung out the side of his mouth, and his legs shook with exertion. Ben was terrified that Hero would get hurt if he had to pull for much longer.

Jack lay down on his back and rolled out of the way.

"I'm out! I'm good!" Jack shouted. "Let it go!"

"Hero, drop it," Ben said. The dog shifted his weight, and Noah and Ben slowly rolled the trunk back down the side of the boulder. "Careful," Ben said to Noah. "A little bit at a time."

Hero moved with them as they lowered the tree. The leash went slack, and Hero dropped down on the soggy ground, panting. Ben stretched out his cramped hands, unsure if he was drenched with rain or sweat.

Jack was safe. They had done it.

Hero had done it.

And now they could go home.

12

BEN DROPPED TO HIS KNEES AND unhooked the leash from Hero's vest. He wrapped his arms around his dog.

"Thank you, buddy," Ben said into Hero's wet fur. "Thank you for saving Jack."

Hero was panting hard. His muscles were shaking from the exertion, and his tongue dangled out of his mouth. They'd been out in the woods and the storm for hours—Ben guessed it had to be close to midnight. Hero hadn't stopped tracking or moving through the dangerous terrain the entire time.

Ben was amazed at his dog's strength and stamina.

Scout scrambled up and over the tree trunk and ran over to Hero. He lay down under Hero's chin and licked the bigger dog's neck and face. Ben reached into his backpack and pulled out his water bottle. He tipped it into Hero's mouth, then Scout's. The dogs lapped up the water.

Noah ran to Jack. "Jack, are you okay?"

Jack lay on the ground, staring up at the trees above him. "I'm fine. I just need a minute to get the blood flowing in my legs again."

"Let me help you," Noah said. He crouched on the ground next to Jack and helped him to a sitting position.

"Thank you," Jack said, putting an arm around Noah's shoulders to hold himself upright. "I mean it—you didn't have to come out here."

Noah shrugged. "What else was I gonna do today?"

Jack smiled. "Fair enough."

"How're your legs?" Noah asked as Jack straightened and bent them a few times.

"Not bad, considering," Jack answered with a grunt.

Noah handed Jack a water bottle, and Jack took a long slug of water.

"You think you can walk?" Ben called over.

"Let me try." Jack eased himself to his feet. Noah reached an arm out to steady him as he took a couple of awkward steps. Jack winced a little. "I'm sore, but nothing's broken or sprained. I'll be fine."

Ben was happy to see Jack up on his feet—and even happier to see his two closest friends getting along.

"You'd better get that leg back in working order before practice starts," Ben joked.

Jack rolled his eyes. "You just worry about your pitching arm," he said. "That should keep you busy till spring."

Ben and Noah laughed. Same old Jack.

Jack shivered. Ben noticed that he was wearing a thin raincoat—not much heavier than a Windbreaker—that was matted to his body with water.

"You must be freezing," Ben said. "Here—I brought your sweatshirt." He tossed Jack's hoodie to him. Jack caught it and looked at it for a second.

"Is this what you—I mean, is this what Hero used to track me?"

"Yup," Ben said, patting Hero on the head.

"I'm sorry, Ben," Jack said, his voice cracking. "I'm a total idiot."

"Well, now you're a total idiot who's been rescued," Ben said.

"Wait, I really mean it," Jack said. "Thank you." He looked at Ben and then Noah. "Seriously, guys, I should have listened. This was the worst idea ever, and I was just—my dad and I used to go camping all the time, so I figured I'd be fine. Plus I really thought they were exaggerating about the hurricane . . ." He trailed off. "This sounds lame considering that you guys just saved my life and Scout's, but . . . thanks."

"You're welcome," Ben and Noah said at the same time. Ben punched Jack lightly on the shoulder.

"You must really miss your dad," Noah said softly. "I had no idea."

"I really do," Jack said with a nod.

"What's he like?" Noah asked.

"He's fun." Jack shrugged. "I don't know—he just— he understands me. My mom is great, don't get me wrong. She's the best. But my dad can make me laugh even when I don't want to. I don't have to explain any-thing to him. He just gets it."

"That's cool," Noah said.

"But since we moved here, I don't get to see him very much. It's kind of hard for me to visit him," Jack said. "He works a lot, you know?"

Ben did know what it was like to have a dad who worked a lot. He flashed on an image of his dad in his police uniform, and suddenly he was struck by an intense urge to head home. Now that Jack and Scout were safe, a wave of worry washed over Ben, and he was anxious to get going. He swallowed a painful lump in his throat. He wanted to see his dad with his own eyes and make sure he was okay. And how badly had Gulfport been hit? Was their house still standing?

Ben wished he could climb a hill and see the town from where they were, but they were way too deep into the woods. He wasn't sure he'd ever been this far into the forest, in fact. He just wanted to get back home quickly, but it was going to be a long trek through some rough conditions.

Every second they were out here was another second when something terrible could happen to his dad—or when his dad could discover that they were gone. And once that happened, Ben thought with a shudder, he knew he was going to be in major trouble.

Ben realized he hadn't checked his phone in a while. He pulled it from the sealed pocket in his rain slicker, where it had been safely stashed. He'd been right about the time—it was 11:50 P.M.

But Ben's stomach plummeted as he looked at the top of the screen. Small letters spelled out NO SERVICE. The storm had probably knocked out cell and Internet service in the entire region. Maybe his dad had already tried to call or text him, but there was no way for Ben to know.

They had to get out of here before the lack of cell service became a real problem.

"Hero, Scout," Ben said, "let's go."

The rain was coming down steadily, but the thunder had subsided—for the moment, at least. If they were lucky and the weather held out a little longer, they might have a shot at getting back before anyone even noticed they were gone.

The dogs got to their feet. Ben was relieved to see that Hero was walking normally and didn't seem like he was in any pain.

Ben hoisted his heavy pack onto his back and stepped over the fallen tree. Jack took a few steps, each one steadier than the last.

"I'll be fine," Jack said in response to the worried look on Ben's face. "Let's get out of here. I'm done with nature for a while."

Ben pulled out his compass and steered the group back in the direction they'd come from.

"Hey, Noah," Jack said.

"Yeah?"

"What color is that outfit you're wearing? Is that pink?"

Ben had forgotten that Noah was wearing his mom's rain gear. He burst out laughing.

"Cute, Jack," Noah snorted. "Who just lifted a forty-million-pound tree off your leg? Should I put it back on top of you?"

"Yeah, good luck with that," Jack said.

Ben used the compass to guide them southwest, but he didn't really need to—Hero knew the way home. They followed the dogs through the debris-strewn forest. Ben felt the ground sloping downhill as they headed back in the direction of town. He stumbled under the weight of his pack, struggling to find his footing in the dark. Exhaustion was slowly starting to set in.

Hero and Scout weaved back and forth just ahead of him, their noses low to the ground, perking up their heads at every sound. Hero led them safely around the swollen river—and the alligator—which added a quarter of a mile or so to their trip. But better to walk a little extra than to see their reptilian enemy again.

They were still about a mile from the edge of the woods when Ben realized they had descended into a small valley, with wooded hills rising on either side of them. Ben regretted not grabbing a map from his dad's supplies. He pulled out his compass and studied it for a second. He tried to remember what he knew about the national park's geography. Based on where he figured they were, Ben thought Hero had picked a good path: If they followed the valley all the way, they would come out of the woods very close to town.

Except for the sound of the rain and steady wind, it was quiet, and the canopy of trees above them was thick. Ben took a deep, slow breath. His nerves started to feel a little less frayed. He just wanted to get home and get into some dry clothes.

Ben turned to say something to Noah and Jack, but before he could speak, an earsplitting *crack!* pierced the air. The sound rattled Ben's teeth. It wasn't a tree falling—it was a bigger, deeper, and scarier sound than that. He looked around frantically for the source of it but couldn't spot anything. Hero had stopped walking and stood on high alert, his muscles twitching, his head and ears up, tuned into sound frequencies the boys couldn't hear.

"What was that?" Noah asked nervously.

"I don't know," Ben said. "But I didn't like the sound of it."

They were silent for a moment, waiting. Listening.

Jack squinted into the darkness, looking into the woods back the way they had come.

"Guys . . ." Jack started to say.

Ben and Noah followed his gaze. Ben couldn't see anything, but he could hear a low sound, like a *whoosh* . . . and it was getting louder. A lot louder.

"Guys!" Jack said, louder this time. "This isn't good."

"What is it?" Ben asked. His heart pounded hard in his chest, and his throat felt constricted.

"I think it's—" Jack paused. Suddenly his eyes grew huge and round. "It's water! *RUN!* Uphill! Now!"

Ben didn't stop to think.

"Hero! Scout! Come!" Ben shouted. He scrambled after Noah and Jack up the hill to their right. The dogs shot up the steep, rocky slope. Ben glanced behind him to see a wall of water barreling through the valley. It was a flash flood.

Rushing toward them at lightning speed was a body of water unlike any Ben had ever seen—tree trunks and boulders spun and somersaulted in the churning white tide, which swallowed everything in its path. The water roared so loudly that Ben's eardrums vibrated.

Ben and the others huddled together just a few

feet above the waterline, clinging to tree roots so that they wouldn't slip down the soggy hill. Water splashed everywhere.

Ben kept his eye on the water level, making sure it wasn't rising any farther toward them. He stayed alert, ready to run uphill if necessary, but it looked as if the river wasn't getting any higher. At least not for the moment.

From his perch, Ben could tell that the water had to be at least six feet deep. Ben was glad they were all safe, but he couldn't believe that the spot where they'd been standing just seconds earlier was now totally submerged. And he knew something that Noah and Jack did not: Their quickest path home was now completely underwater.

13

NOAH FOUND HIS VOICE FIRST. "THAT was close."

"A little too close." Jack shook his head.

Below them, the valley had been completely destroyed in the flood.

"We can't go back down there," Noah said, pointing at the rapidly moving water.

"We have to find another way home," Ben said. "You guys stay here. I'm going to see what's at the top of the hill. Hero, come."

Ben slogged up the muddy slope while Hero darted ahead of him. Hero paused at the top and looked back at Ben, waiting. The wind and rain were stronger up there, but there was just enough faint moonlight breaking through the gray clouds for Ben to see in all four directions.

To his left, the ridge angled upward, narrowing at the top and zigzagging to the east and west—a winding route that would add a mile or more to their trip home. And with the sludgy, wet ground and scattered debris, the path would be dangerous—and maybe even impossible.

Ben knew what he needed to do. His stomach churned, but there wasn't much choice. Ben pulled out his phone and swiped at it. They needed help.

He had to call his dad.

One look at his phone, though, and the pit in Ben's stomach got worse.

There was still no signal.

They were stuck, and it was all Ben's fault.

They had no way to get back, and no way to tell anyone where they were. And now, Ben realized, this wasn't just about getting busted for going out in the hurricane. This was about their parents not knowing where they were—and whether they were okay. The last thing Ben wanted to do was make his dad worry.

Ben had to get his friends home. But now he could only see one way out—and that was to go straight up.

"Hey, guys," he called down to Noah and Jack. He gestured for them to join him. They headed up, Scout following. Ben noticed that Jack was limping a little as he climbed the slippery hill.

"What's up?" Noah asked, huffing and puffing as he summited the hill and stood next to Ben. Scout leaned out and sniffed around the edge.

"Do either of your phones work?" Ben asked.

"Mine's soaking wet," Jack said sheepishly.

Noah pulled his from his pocket. It was dry, but, like Ben, he had no signal bars.

Ben racked his brain for a minute, trying to figure out what to do next. They were in a tough spot and his friends were counting on him. Finally, Ben said, "I have a plan." He jabbed a thumb over his shoulder, toward the skinny path that led upward. "We're going that way."

Noah groaned.

"Yikes," Jack said.

"I know. It's not pretty," Ben said, "but we need to get a cell signal. And unfortunately heading up and out of the forest is the only way to do that."

"All right, then," Noah said, "let's start climbing."

It was going to be a long hike. It had taken them hours to get this far, and it was going to take even longer to get back. Plus, they were exhausted—it was well after midnight—and Jack was injured. As Noah passed around a few granola bars, Ben bent over and picked up a long, thin tree branch. He handed it to Jack. "Maybe this'll work like a cane?"

"Thanks," Jack said, hefting the stick in his hand. He stuck the pointed end into the mud, leaned on it, and took a step forward. "Perfect."

The boys fell into a single-file line and began walking up the steep hill. They lifted their boots out of the heavy mud, then plunged them down again, step by step. Noah kept pace in front, then Jack, and Ben brought up the rear. Hero and Scout darted around their legs, sniffing at the terrain. It was hard work, and for a long while no one spoke.

Every few minutes, Ben checked his phone. Still no service. He hadn't said this to Noah and Jack, but he wasn't *entirely* sure going higher would get them any closer to a cell tower signal. It was possible service in the entire area was out. Either way, based on that flash flood, Ben figured getting to higher ground wouldn't be a bad thing.

They kept walking. There was no sound except the suctioning of their boots. This couldn't have been further from how they usually spent their Friday nights. They normally threw a ball around, watched a movie, or went to a friend's house. And by midnight, Ben would be in his room with Hero, falling asleep while watching baseball videos on YouTube . . . which sounded pretty good right now.

Ben stared down at his feet, looking for tripping hazards and sharp drops off the side.

"Take your time, Noah," Jack joked from his spot in the middle of the pack. "It's cool. We're not in a hurry."

"Seriously?" Noah stopped and spun around to face Jack.

"Dude," Jack held up both hands in front of him. "I was just messing with you."

"Well, it's not funny," Noah snapped back.

Ben was surprised by the level of irritation in his friends' voices. "Guys—it's cool," he called from the back. Noah and Jack had just started getting along at last, and he wanted it to stick. "We're all a little fried. Can we just keep going?"

"Fine," Noah grumbled.

"Yeah, sure. Whatever," Jack said.

The ground started to level off. Ben hoped they had reached the summit, at least, so the trek would get a little easier. He sighed and checked his phone. There was the flicker of a bar—Ben's chest fluttered with hope.

Then, from up ahead, there was a *thunk*, a grunt, and a series of pained cries. Ben looked up to see Noah on the ground, with Jack half sitting, half lying on top of him.

"Dude!" Noah snapped.

"Sorry—I tripped."

"Can you get off me, please?"

"Noah—I'm sorry. It was an accident."

"Guys!" Ben interrupted them.

"Were your eyes even open?" Noah went on. "Because I'm right in front of you."

"Guys! Stop it!" Ben tried again. "I have service!"

Noah and Jack forgot their argument and hurried over. Ben held up his phone to show them the single signal bar. He hoped it was enough.

His fingers were puckered and cold, but he managed to swipe at his phone and tap his dad's number. Ben lifted the phone to his ear and held his breath.

There was silence on the line while it tried to connect. Ben waited, his heart pounding in his chest. Noah and Jack watched his face hopefully.

He pulled the phone away from his ear and looked

at the screen. CONNECTING, the screen read.

The boys held their breath. Even Hero and Scout sat still at their feet, waiting.

Ben lifted the phone to his ear again. Still, nothing happened.

The call wouldn't go through.

Ben tapped the red button to disconnect. He typed out a quick text to his dad to see if it would send. No luck. He tried an e-mail. Again, nothing.

Noah and Jack turned away. Each of the boys stood by himself for a few seconds.

Finally, Ben spoke.

"Let's keep moving," he said. "We need to get home."

14

THE WIND GUSTED AND HOWLED. THE boys planted their feet firmly on the uneven path and kept their balance as best they could, while the dogs moved steadily ahead.

The ridge had flattened into a path, with woods spreading out on either side of them. The ground was soaked but not flooded. Hero brushed against Ben's leg as they walked. Ben reached down and ran his fingers through the fur on Hero's back.

Suddenly, Hero froze mid-step, and Ben felt the dog's body tense. Ben stopped short and watched Hero, who stared off into the woods, his ears and tail up.

"What is it, buddy?" Ben asked. Hero's ear twitched

at the sound of Ben's voice. They all stood in silence, waiting.

Hero shot off so fast that Ben didn't even have time to call out his name. Hero disappeared into the darkness of the trees in the blink of an eye. At Jack's side, Scout went nuts—he barked and howled frantically.

"Scout, stay," Jack commanded him. Scout scurried back and forth along the tree line, but he didn't go after Hero.

"Hero!" Ben called into the woods. Shock and frustration rattled his nerves. "Hero, come back!"

But there was no sign of his dog. Ben felt close to panic. His heart pounded in his chest. It wasn't like Hero to disappear like that—was something wrong with him? "What do we do?" Ben asked Noah and Jack.

"How can we follow him if we can't even see where he went?" Noah asked.

"Scout can lead us," Jack said. "Right, Scout?"

"Is he ready for that?" Noah asked.

"I've been working with him," Jack said. "And Ben and his dad are always telling me he's a natural search-and-rescue dog."

"You're right," Ben agreed. "Scout's good. He's our best chance of catching up with Hero."

"Sounds good to me," Noah said, giving Scout a scratch behind his ears. The puppy wagged his tail, ready to go.

"Scout, find Hero!" Jack said firmly. Without a moment's hesitation, Scout ran into the woods, following Hero's scent.

Scout darted around trees, his nose to the ground. He hurtled forward, his front and back legs tucking under him with every stride. Ben had never seen Scout so focused—it was like he had suddenly become a real search dog.

The boys tried to keep up, the mud pulling at their boots and slowing them down. Noah slipped on the slick ground, and Jack stopped to give him a hand. Noah grabbed it, and Jack pulled him to his feet. They took off running again, Jack with a slight limp.

"Hero!" Ben called out. A hundred or so yards up ahead, Ben saw the flicker of Hero's reflective vest in the moonlight. "There!" he shouted to Noah and Jack.

The boys panted and hurried after Scout, deeper into the woods. In the back of his mind, Ben sensed they were heading farther from home.

They must have jogged for half a mile before Scout finally led them up a small hill. Scout stopped at the top,

113

and the boys gathered around him, catching their breath. Scout sniffed at the ground, then started to head down the opposite side. The boys exchanged skeptical glances before following the puppy.

Ben stopped in his tracks when he saw a low opening in the other side of the hill. It was the mouth of a cave. And there, in the entrance, stood Hero.

"Hero, what are you doing?" Ben said angrily as he tried to leash his dog. He'd never spoken to Hero like that before—but Hero had never run off like that either. Hero dodged out of Ben's hands and trotted into the cave. "Hero, stop!" Ben said. But the dog ignored him.

Ben and Scout followed close behind Hero. Noah and Jack brought up the rear, both letting out deep, exhausted sighs.

The cave opened into a large cavern. It was so much bigger than Ben expected—he couldn't see the back of it. Ben turned on his flashlight and followed Hero farther and farther in, until he saw, in the dim light, what Hero was heading for.

People.

"Who's there?" a man's voice called out.

"Um, hi," Noah replied. "We got lost."

"We're from Gulfport," Ben added.

Ben aimed his flashlight on a small group of people sitting around a lantern—a man and several boys in Boy Scout uniforms. The kids were younger than Ben, maybe seven or eight years old. As Ben got closer to them, glimmers of hope and relief crossed their faces. Except for the Boy Scout leader—he looked like he was in some serious pain.

The man leaned back against the rock wall, his eyes squeezed shut, his face pale and glistening with sweat. His leg stuck out in front of him at a weird angle. Ben could tell that it was broken. Noah, Ben, and Jack ran over and crouched down next to him.

"Are you okay, sir?" Ben asked, though he already knew the answer.

The Boy Scout leader opened his eyes just enough to squint at Ben.

"I'm Marco."

"Nice to meet you, Marco," Ben said. "What happened to your leg?"

"It's broken. A branch fell and knocked me down a hill. Broke it on the way down." Marco sounded like every word was painful, and he was trying to use as few as possible.

"How long have you been out here?" Jack asked.

"We've been camping for three days. I don't understand where that storm came from—I checked the forecast over and over before we left. It wasn't supposed to be nearly that bad. I was prepared for some rain, but this . . ." He trailed off and winced.

"That wasn't just a storm," Ben said. "It was a hurricane. It changed course at the last minute today—there wasn't any time to evacuate or anything."

"That explains why my radio's out," Marco said. "I feel terrible for putting these boys in danger. Their parents must be worried sick."

"Well," Ben said reassuringly, "it looks like you kept them safe in here."

Marco closed his eyes and rested his head back against the wall. "How bad is it out there?"

Ben shook his head. "It's pretty rough."

Marco tipped his head toward the back of the cave and whispered, "Well, it isn't good in here either. The water is rising in the back. Fast. The boys haven't noticed it yet, but they will soon. The cave is going to flood—my guess is in the next couple of hours. You need to get them out of here."

Ben peered into the darkness along the far wall of the cave, but he couldn't see anything from where they were.

The thought of rising water made him nervous. He'd seen how quickly things could change out in the woods, especially when it came to water.

"What about you?" Ben asked.

"Just take the kids," Marco said. "Then send back help."

"Okay, sir, we can do that," Ben replied.

"Thank you."

Ben looked around at the scared faces of the kids. They definitely had their work cut out for them now. It had been hard enough leading his friends through the woods, but if anyone was cut out for the job, it was Hero and Scout. He gave his dog a rub behind the ears—his way of apologizing for raising his voice at Hero earlier. If it weren't for Hero, these kids might never have been rescued. Hero licked Ben's hand, as if he understood what Ben was trying to say.

"You guys really found a great place to hide out from the storm." Noah tried his best to sound cheerful. The young boys nodded uncertainly.

"Is the storm over?" one of the Boy Scouts said in a high, shaky voice.

"Almost," Ben said. The boys stared back at him with big, round eyes. He scrambled for the right thing to say but came up blank. "Uh, my name is Ben." He gave them a quick wave. "And these are my two friends, Jack and Noah."

The Boy Scouts just stared at the older boys, until Hero and Scout ambled over to the group and sniffed at their dirt-caked uniforms. Smiles broke out on the kids' faces as they reached out to pet the dogs.

"Excuse me, mister," a Boy Scout with thick glasses and big cheeks called out to Ben. The boy was pointing at Hero. "Isn't this the dog from the TV news? The police dog who saves lives?"

Ben grinned.

"That's him," he said.

"What's his name?" the boy asked.

"Hero," Ben replied. "His name is Hero. And he's going to get you all home."

15

A SKINNY DARK-HAIRED BOY RAN TO Marco and gave him a hug. "Dad," the boy said. His eyes were puffy from crying. "I'm not leaving you here."

"It's okay, Cory," Marco said. "You just need to get out of here, and then you can send someone back for me."

"No, Dad—"

Marco struggled to lift his arm and put it around Cory's shoulders. With a grimace, he pulled his son in close. "I'm okay, buddy. I just need to know that you're going to get home safe."

Cory burst into tears and buried his face in his dad's shirt. Marco stroked his son's head.

"Ben," Marco called, his voice hoarse. "Do you have a cell phone?"

Ben nodded. "But there's no service. We were on our way to higher ground."

"When you get a signal, call for help. Once the boys are safe—and only after they're safe—send someone for me," Marco said.

Ben shook his head. "We can't just leave you here—"

"Please, Ben," Marco cut him off. "Take care of Cory and the others. Please?"

Ben studied the man's face. He recognized something in his expression—a look he'd seen on his own dad's face many times. It was conviction. Marco believed this was the best solution for his own son, and for all the other boys too.

"I will," Ben said. "And we'll be back for you."

"Take this map," Marco said, handing Ben a neatly folded rectangle of paper. "I marked where we are right now. And take this too." He handed Ben a walkie-talkie. "I'll keep the other. They've got a long range, so when the signal's back, we should be able to talk. Let me know that you're safe and help is on the way—and that Cory's okay." Marco's voice cracked a little.

Ben slipped the walkie-talkie into his pocket. He

clutched the map in his palm. Marco closed his eyes and rested his head against the wall again.

Ben turned to the boys and clapped his hands together, trying to rally some energy. "Raise your hand," he said, his voice light and encouraging, "if you're ready to get a little wet!"

"We can't leave our leader," the boys cried. Cory's eyes filled with tears.

"We're not leaving him for long," Jack said, resting next to the boys. "We're going to let him relax for a few minutes while we go get help."

"Yeah," Noah chimed in, "actually, he really needs us to hurry so we can call someone to come and get him. The faster we go, the faster he'll get some help. Okay?"

The Boy Scouts nodded.

"It's okay, guys," Marco said, mustering as much strength as he could, his voice as cheerful as he could make it sound. "Go on ahead. Just make sure whoever you send brings me a nice hot cheeseburger, okay?"

The Boy Scouts scrambled to their feet, still uncertain but doing what they were told. Hero and Scout stood up too.

"Besides," Ben said, "you're not just going to get help. You're hiking through the woods with Gulfport's famous search-and-rescue dog!" The kids broke into weak smiles. "Come, Hero," Ben said. Hero walked to him. "Sit." Hero sat. The boys were frozen, their eyes locked on Hero. Ben paused for effect. "Hero, go!"

Hero bolted across the cave. He looked so official— almost regal—in his yellow vest. The boys were mesmerized.

"Hero, stop!"

Hero stopped almost instantaneously. The kids opened their mouths in awe.

Ben had been working on a new trick with Hero, just for fun. He hadn't shown it to anyone yet, but this was as good a time as any.

"Hero, dance!"

Hero trotted toward Ben, bobbing his head up and down and doing a funny little skittering step.

The kids—and Noah and Jack—burst out laughing.

"Good boy, Hero!" Ben dropped to his knees and hugged his dog. "What do you think, guys? You ready to follow Hero and go home?"

"Yes!" the boys cheered. They pulled their packs onto their tiny shoulders and formed a line, ready to go. Cory knelt down to give his dad a hug, and then, his eyes damp, he joined the others.

"Hero, let's go!" Ben called out. Hero sauntered to the mouth of the cave and stopped. He stood with his head held high, his jet-black fur glistening, all his muscles flexed, and his tail pointed up, ready for his next command.

Ben looked back at Marco, who gave him a thumbs-up.

Ben gave him a salute and said, "We'll be back soon."

16

THEY MARCHED IN A SINGLE-FILE LINE as the hurricane wound down around them. The weather was calmer, although the wind still shook the trees high above the boys, and the rain came steadily down on them. Ben kept checking his phone, waiting for a signal. The clock said it was close to four in the morning.

Hero led the way, with Ben right behind him. Before they'd left the cave, Noah had clipped Hero's and Scout's leashes together to create a long tether. Each of the little boys gripped the nylon rope with one mud-caked hand as they marched. This kept them all in a row and prevented anyone from wandering off the path.

Noah positioned himself in the middle of the pack, with three Boy Scouts in front of him and four behind him. Jack and Scout brought up the rear. Every time one of the kids started to lag, Scout ran up and nudged him with his nose, urging him along.

They followed Marco's map. The path angled uphill again. Ben leaned forward, pushing himself as the road got harder and his legs got more tired. He looked over his shoulder. The Boy Scouts pursed their lips and furrowed their brows, concentrating hard on getting up the hill. They looked so young and scared—but none of them complained. They just wanted to get home.

Cory was right behind Ben. He was trying really hard not to cry—and mostly, he was succeeding. Ben couldn't imagine leaving his own dad behind, hurt and trapped like that.

A pang of fear shot through Ben's chest as he thought about Dad. Did he even know Ben was missing—and was he worried about him? Either way, Ben hoped that he'd find out the answer soon.

Off in the distance, Ben heard the sound of a creek running. It was heavy and fast-moving, probably overflowing with rainwater. He shined his flashlight on the map. Eventually they were going to have to cross that creek in order to get to higher ground—and closer to Gulfport.

Cory sniffled and choked back a sob. Ben stopped walking and let Cory catch up. He put his hand on the boy's shoulder and squeezed. "It's gonna be okay," Ben said, hoping he was right. "Just picture your dad doing something really fun that you love to do together. And only think of that."

"Okay," Cory muttered.

Hero darted around their legs, and Cory smiled a little through his tears.

Ben had an idea. "Hey," he called out to the others, "you guys want to hear about one of Hero's big rescues back when he was a police dog?" No one answered at first.

Then a soft voice from the middle of the pack said, "Yes, please."

There were so many great Hero rescue stories—Ben racked his brain for just the right one.

He could tell them the one about how he'd gotten lost in the woods when he was just a little boy— younger than these Boy Scouts were. Ben had been terrified and convinced he'd never see his parents again. But Hero had come racing out of the darkness and found him crying, alone, under a tree.

That was Ben's personal favorite, of course.

Or he could tell them how Hero had tracked a bank robber by sniffing a single piece of paper that the crook had touched. He'd followed the man's scent from the bank, down the street, through an office building, and into the basement where he was hiding.

But nope. Ben knew which story he would tell the Boy Scouts.

"Have you guys heard about the Front Porch Robber?" Ben asked.

"My mom told me about him," said a boy, Jonah, from the middle of the pack. "She said he was weird."

Ben laughed. "Yeah, he was weird. 'Cause he really liked taking weird stuff. A few years ago, people started noticing that their things were disappearing from their front porches at night."

"Like what?" asked Jonah.

"Like, he stole a rocking chair once. And another time he just took a potted plant."

"What?"

"No way!"

"Why would anyone take a plant?"

The boys were giggling now.

"Who knows why, but this guy took a plant," Ben went on. "And a tricycle. And even—are you ready for this?"

"Yes!" the boys cackled.

"A chicken!" Ben shouted.

The boys were laughing so hard they had to stop walking for a second.

"Anyway," Ben said, tugging on the tether to get them moving again, "no one could catch the Front Porch Robber. Not the cops. Not the neighbors. No one. Until . . ."

The boys went totally silent. Ben let them wait until they couldn't take it for a second longer.

"Until what?" they yelled.

"What do you think?" Ben asked. He waved a hand in Hero's direction.

"Hero caught him!" the boys cried.

"That's right. Hero caught him. One night in the middle of the night, a woman saw the robber running away from her house." Ben lowered his voice and spoke slowly, dramatically, drawing out the story. "And she called the police right away. So they knew that the guy had just been there. My dad and Hero got to her house a few minutes later, and they found a glove the thief dropped when he ran away. He'd never left anything behind before, so this was a big deal."

"Then what happened?" one boy, Emmett, asked.

"But the robber was gone already," another boy, Isaiah, said. "How could Hero find him? Could he see him?"

"Nope," Ben said, "but he could smell him. Just like he can smell you right now. Did you know that everyone has their own smell? It comes from little pieces of your skin that fly off you."

"Gross!" The boys giggled.

"It sounds gross, but it's really cool, actually," Ben said. "You and I can't smell each other so much. But Hero knows the difference between each and every one of us, because his sense of smell is thousands of times better than ours. Crazy, right?"

"So he could smell the bad guy or what?" Emmett asked impatiently.

"You got it. Hero knew the thief's smell from the glove. Then he sniffed the ground and the air and the grass and the dirt, and he found the guy's smell on all those things too. And he followed it really far. And do you know where they found the Front Porch Robber?"

"Where?!" the boys cried out all at once.

"In a trash can."

"For real?" Emmett asked, suspicious.

"For real," Ben said. "He was hiding in someone's trash can outside their house. He had put the lid on over his head and everything. But Hero smelled him and signaled to my dad where he was. And they caught him."

"Wow."

"Cool."

"Didn't the trash smell really bad?"

"Yeah." Ben laughed. "I'm guessing it smelled really bad. But that didn't stop you, right, Hero?"

Hero wagged his tail, almost as if he knew the story was about him.

17

THEY WERE MAKING GOOD PROGRESS, BUT as they neared the top of the hill, the path abruptly narrowed to no more than two feet wide. The ground dropped off sharply to their left and sloped steeply upward to their right. Ben's pack brushed against the roots and branches that stuck out from the wall of earth next to him.

Ben told the boys to be careful while they stepped sideways along the treacherous path. Scout and Hero yipped and howled encouragement.

Soon they arrived on the bank of the creek, although it looked more like a raging river—it was churning with debris from the hurricane. Ben and Hero stopped, and the group came to a halt behind them.

"Uh," Jack said quietly so the boys couldn't hear, "where's the bridge?"

According to the map in Ben's hand, it was supposed to be right where they were standing.

Ben double-checked the coordinates on his compass. This was the spot.

"That *is* the bridge," he said, pointing to what was left of it: some old lumber lying across the creek, partly submerged in the water, with a busted railing leaning off of one side—and one side only. The other side was long gone, probably miles downstream by then. The bridge bobbed up and down with the current.

"Oh, man," Noah exhaled. He looked nervously over his shoulder at the kids and their heavy backpacks. "How are we going to get them over that?"

Ben stepped closer to the water to investigate. He put one foot on the wood and pushed down hard. It wobbled and bounced, but it was still firmly attached to its concrete base. As long as the wood itself held out, they should be able to make it.

Ben walked back to Noah and Jack and sighed. "Very carefully," he said.

Within a few minutes, Ben, Noah, and Jack had come up with a pretty good plan for getting across. But they would have to go one at a time.

Noah was first. The tether he had created with the dogs' leashes was more than long enough to reach across the creek. Ben tied it tightly around Noah's waist, weaving it through Noah's belt loops. There was no way it would come off.

Then Ben clipped the other end to Hero's collar. Hero would stay on the bank while Noah made his way—slowly—across the bridge. If Noah fell, Hero was strong enough to pull him back up onto the bank.

"You ready?" Ben asked.

Noah nodded but didn't speak. He took the first step onto the wood. It sagged under his weight, and he grimaced. He took another step. Then another. The bridge dipped and bowed as he tread across it carefully. The water ran over the tops of his boots.

Ben and Jack stood on either side of Hero, their hands on the tether for backup. Ben forced himself to inhale, then exhale. Inhale, exhale. Noah took a few more steps. He gripped what was left of the railing for balance.

The bridge held. Noah stepped onto the muddy ground on the other side. "Whoop!" he yelled, his fist punching the air in victory.

"Nice work!" Ben yelled.

"Go, Noah!" Jack shouted.

The Boy Scouts cheered in unison.

Noah untied the tether from his waist and found a strong tree on the far bank. He tied that end of the leash to it. Now the boys would have something other than the railing to hold on to.

"Okay, guys, line up single file," Jack called out to them. The boys did as they were told.

Jonah went first. He bit his lower lip and focused, hard, on putting one foot in front of the other.

"Don't look down!" Noah urged him from the other side. "Look at me." Jonah lifted his gaze and locked eyes with Noah. "That's right, buddy. One foot in front of the other. You got it."

Jonah looked tiny under his giant backpack, his skinny arms held out to the sides for balance. When he reached the middle of the bridge, he hesitated over the churning water for a moment. Then he forged ahead. When he made it to the other side, he jumped into Noah's arms in triumph.

Emmett was next. Then Isaiah. All the while, Hero stood firmly in the mud, his muscles flexed as he braced the tether with his body.

Ben unhooked the tether from Hero's collar as he prepared to tie the cord around a boy named Diego's waist. As he did, Hero raised his head and cocked it to the side. His ears shot up, he sniffed at the air, and he stared upstream, into the distance. Ben knew his dog's posture could only mean one thing: Hero was tuned into something they couldn't hear or see yet. The hair on Ben's arms stood on end.

Jack had noticed it too. And so had Cory.

Cory stood close to Ben. He turned his tearstained face up to look Ben in the eye.

"What is it?" Cory asked quietly, so the other boys couldn't hear.

"I don't know," Ben said truthfully. "But Hero senses something. Hero—what is it, boy?"

Hero didn't wait around for Ben to figure out the answer. He sprinted toward the remaining four boys, who were spread out along the bank, waiting nervously for their turn to cross the river. He ran in circles around them, slowly pushing them into a tight cluster next to Ben.

"He's herding them," Jack said to Ben.

"Yeah," Ben said. "But why?"

The Boy Scouts' faces were suddenly tight with worry.

Hero ran back and forth between them and the water's edge. He barked ferociously, repeating the movement and the sound over and over.

Finally it clicked. Ben knew what Hero was trying to tell them.

"We're out of time," Ben whispered to Jack. "I don't know why, but we have to get out of here." He turned to the kids. "Okay, boys," he said evenly but firmly, trying to keep the fear he felt out of his voice. "We need to double-time this, okay? That means we can't go one at a time anymore."

Ben handed the end of the leash to Jack.

"Jack, wrap that around their waists and thread it through their belt loops. It should be long enough."

Jack nodded and got to work. The tether was just long enough to attach to the four boys. Ben and Jack were going to have to go across without any safety rope. Jack would go first, with Scout in his arms, then the boys, then Ben.

And Hero was going to have to go last.

Ben studied Hero's body language. The dog was still poised for action, still gazing upstream.

Ben listened carefully to the various sounds of the forest—rain plinking on the ground, creek water bubbling and sloshing, leaves rustling in the trees, the Boy Scouts breathing heavily. At first he heard nothing out of the ordinary, but then, finally, he picked up on a low hum, a steady *whoosh*. It was heading downstream, toward them. And it was getting louder. Fast.

What was it?

"Let's go, guys," Ben said, his encouraging tone just barely masking the terror that was rising in him.

Jack stepped onto the bridge and turned around to offer his hand to Will. Will put one shaky foot onto the wooden plank. Jack walked backward, with Noah coaching him from the other side. The boys on the far bank watched them silently, their eyes big and round with worry.

Diego stepped up next, then Nicholas and Cory. The boys shuffled nervously across, the wood dipping a few inches into the water under their weight. They slipped and started to stumble, but Jack steadied them.

"You're doing great, guys," Ben urged them on from his spot next to Hero.

The sound was getting louder.

They had to hurry.

The group was halfway across the bridge when Ben

heard Cory crying. The boy had frozen in his tracks, too scared to go any farther.

"You got this, Cory," Ben shouted. "You're almost there. Just a few more feet."

"I'm scared!" Cory let out a loud sob. The boys next to him started to cry too, their shoulders shaking.

"Your dad needs you to keep moving, okay, Cory?" Ben begged him. "We have to go get help so we can go back and get him, remember?"

That did the trick. Cory still looked miserable, but he sucked in his breath and took one step. Then another. The boys were moving again.

Ben didn't have time to feel relief. Suddenly he felt the first stinging sprays of something small and sharp hitting his face and head. It was like a sandstorm—but it wasn't sand. It was wet and dirty. He wiped his cheek and looked at his hand. It was gritty mud, and it seemed to suddenly fill the air around them.

Ben looked upstream, and that's when he saw it.

It was a mudslide.

An oozing, spreading, seething layer of mud, gurgling straight down the creek, spilling over the banks on either side and picking up rocks and splintered tree branches as it moved. It was gaining in volume and strength and swallowing up the creek, making everything in its path simply disappear.

The mud looked alive, and it was moving quickly. Too quickly. They only had a few seconds left before it washed out the bridge entirely, taking the entire group with it.

"GO!" Ben shouted at the boys and Jack. "Go go go go go!"

On the other end of the leash, Hero held his ground. He dug his paws into the mud and crouched as low as he could, steadying the boys. Ben stood next to him, holding on to the rope too.

"Come on come on come on!" Noah shouted. Finally, Jack, Scout, and the rest of the kids tumbled onto land. Noah quickly untied the leash from the tree and began detaching them from it. The kids scurried out of the path of the mudslide as quickly as they could.

"Ben, Hero! Let's go!" Jack shouted.

Ben looked anxiously toward the mud. It was only a few feet away. They had to move. *Now.*

"Hero, go!" Ben commanded. Hero and Ben leaped off the muddy bank at the same moment, landing halfway across the bridge. They raced to the other side just in time.

With incredible power, the wall of mud blasted into the bridge, ripping it from its posts and tossing it into the air. Within seconds, the bridge had disappeared under the sludge.

Ben lay on the ground, catching his breath. He was shaking. Hero came over and licked the mud off Ben's face.

Noah fell to the ground next to him and let out a long, loud "Whew."

"You can say that again," Ben said. He wanted desperately to rest, but there was no time. He got to his feet. "Everyone okay?" he asked the Boy Scouts.

Seven little heads nodded.

Ben pulled his phone from his pocket. Still no reception. Noah checked his phone too. Nothing there either.

"We have to keep moving," Noah said.

Ben nodded. He looked up at the tops of the trees for a moment, enjoying the feel of the solid ground beneath his feet. Today, he had already bested an alligator, a flood, and now a mudslide. What was the hurricane going to throw at them next?

Whatever it was, they'd have to be ready for it.

18

THE RAIN HAD STOPPED, THE SKY above them had cleared, and what looked like a million stars lit up the night. It was beautiful.

"Look up, guys," Ben said to the Boy Scouts as they made their way up a hill. The kids let out a refrain of "Wow!" and "Cool!" Some of them looked like they were walking in their sleep. They stumbled and leaned on each other, their eyes half closed. Hero and Scout nudged their legs, trying to keep the boys moving.

Poor kids, Ben thought. He was tired to the very core—even his bones were exhausted. His backpack felt twice as heavy as it had before. He couldn't imagine how the little dudes were handling this.

Just when Ben thought they weren't going to be able to go a single step farther, though, he saw a welcome sight: the top of the ridge.

"We made it to the top!" he hollered. The kids cheered. Somehow they mustered up the energy, and together they ran the last few yards to a large clearing at the hill's summit.

The Boy Scouts dropped to the ground in relief. They put their heads on their backpacks and sprawled out.

Ben, Jack, and Noah walked to the edge of the clearing. There was just enough moonlight for them to see the land around them.

The entire forest was in ruins. Trees were down everywhere. Water flooded where there had been dry land just that morning. There were no animals—everything was still and silent. And in the distance, Ben saw the silhouette of Gulfport. His town—the only place he had ever lived. The city was dark. All the power must have been knocked out.

Before Ben could fully process what he was seeing, his phone buzzed in his pocket. His phone! It was working! Hero nosed at Ben's pocket and licked Ben's hand.

Ben snatched the phone out of his jacket and cheered at the text and voice mail notifications that popped up on his screen. Now that he had service again, everything from the last few hours was coming through at once. Ben didn't stop to read or listen to anything. He swiped at the screen and quickly dialed his dad's number.

"Ben!" his dad answered. "Ben, is that you? Are you okay? Where are you? I've been trying to reach you."

"Hi, Dad. I'm fine—" Ben's chest swelled with emotion at the sound of his dad's voice. He ran a hand through Hero's soft fur to steady himself. "I'm fine—Noah and Jack are okay too. We're together—and—and we have a Boy Scout troop with us—I'll explain later."

"A Boy Scout troop?" his dad asked, surprised. "Seven kids? Is their leader named Marco?"

"Yeah," Ben replied. "Have you been looking for them?"

His dad let out a short laugh. "Yeah, we've been looking for them, Ben. Really hard. I'm so happy you're with them. Are they all okay?"

"Their troop leader—he's got a broken leg and he's back in a cave. Someone has to go get him. We've got his radio so you can find him," Ben said.

Ben looked over at Cory, who watched him anxiously. Ben gave the boy a thumbs-up, and Cory broke into a tentative smile.

"Now tell me—where are you guys?" Ben's dad asked.

Ben's stomach dropped out. This was the part he had been dreading—the part where he had to confess to his dad that he had gone against his word and left the house in the middle of a hurricane.

"Ben?"

"We're—um—I guess we're sort of—in the woods. The national forest. I'll text you my location, okay?"

There was silence on the other end of the line. Ben heard the buzz of a chaotic police station in the background. People shouted and phones rang. But his dad said nothing for a moment.

"Send it to me now, son," his dad finally said, his voice heavy. "I'll be right there. Are you safe where you are?"

"Yes, Dad," Ben said, deeply grateful that his dad hadn't asked any questions. For now, at least. "We're fine."

"Stay right where you are. We're on our way. And, Ben—" His dad's voice cracked.

"Yeah, Dad?"

"I love you, buddy."

"I love you too, Dad. And I'm so sorry."

His dad sighed into the phone.

"Let's just get you home, son. Okay?"

"Okay."

Ben hung up and quickly opened his GPS app. He sent his dad their coordinates, then pulled out Marco's radio and tried to make contact.

"Marco, can you hear me?" Ben said into the device. The airwaves crackled. "We're safe. Help is on the way."

There was static, then, "Thank you, Ben," Marco replied. Cory's eyes filled with tears at the sound of his dad's voice.

"Are you okay?" Ben asked. He turned away so Cory couldn't hear Marco's response.

"I'm fine," Marco said. "The water hasn't reached me yet. I think the rain must have slowed down."

"We should save the battery," Ben said into his walkie-talkie.

"Ben?" Marco replied, his voice cracking. "Can you tell Cory I love him, and I'll see him real soon?"

"You bet, Marco. I'll tell him right now."

Ben slid the radio into his backpack and turned to Cory. He whispered his dad's message into the boy's ear. Cory smiled and swallowed his tears, then ran off to sit with his friends.

Ben checked the time on his phone. It was five in the morning. For the first time since they'd left the house all those hours ago, Ben felt like everything was going to be okay.

19

THE ADRENALINE WORE OFF QUICKLY. HELP was on the way, but the little kids were wet, freezing cold, and scared—and that's all they could think about. It had started to rain again—not as heavily as before, but enough to remind them that they had been soaked and chilly for hours.

As they sat and waited, the reality of what they had just been through settled in. One by one, the Boy Scouts started to shiver and cry.

Cory was in the worst shape.

"Is my dad still going to be okay?" he asked Ben, his face a mask of worry, his eyes filled with giant tears.

"He's fine, bud—he's fine. And my dad is a cop. He'll be here any minute with a bunch of officers, and they're going to go get your dad right away, okay?"

Cory nodded through his tears. He swallowed hard.

"When are they coming?" asked Jonah, whose dark wet hair was stuck to his face. "I'm freezing. And hungry."

"They'll be here really soon," Ben said. "Just a few minutes. Can you hang on for a few more minutes?" He tried not to sound as desperate as he felt. They'd already divided up all the food Marco had given them and everything they'd brought with them. Granola bars and trail mix didn't go that far for ten people. He really hoped his dad and his team would get there . . . fast.

"What's all this crying?" Noah suddenly said, hopping up from the ground. He made an exaggerated horrified expression. "How can you all sit there feeling sorry for yourselves when there's baseball to be played?"

What was Noah talking about? Ben wondered. Baseball? Here? On the top of a giant hill? With what?

Noah thrust his hands in the air and waved them around. He held a baseball in one hand and wore a mitt on the other. The rain fell on his outstretched arms.

Ben and Jack burst out laughing.

"Have you had your mitt and ball with you all this time?" Ben asked Noah.

Noah just shrugged. "You never know when you might need them." He looked over at the little kids. "Like now—right, guys?"

The Boy Scouts looked at him like he was crazy. They sniffled and wiped their noses on their arms.

But Noah wasn't taking no for an answer.

"You four," he said, waving his mitt at Cory, Emmett, Nicholas, and Jonah. "You guys are on my team. Up and at 'em."

Reluctantly, the kids got up and clustered around Noah.

"And you three," Noah said to the remaining boys on the ground. "You're with those two yokels." He gestured at Ben and Jack. "Sorry, kids, but they're all we've got."

"Hey!" Jack laughed. He looked at his three new, tiny teammates. "Are we gonna let him talk about us like that, or are we gonna show them how the game is played?"

The boys giggled.

"We're gonna smoke 'em," Isaiah said in a squeaky little voice. "That's what we're gonna do."

"Whaaaaaat?!" Noah laughed. He looked at his team. "Let's do this—huh, guys?"

"Yeah!" the kids responded.

The two teams quickly fell into position. Noah put his backpack down as home plate. Ben and Jack used theirs—and Ben's baseball cap—as the bases.

"Cory, you're up!" Noah called out.

Cory picked up the long tree branch they were using as a bat and raised it above his head. The branch bobbed behind him, and he crouched into a perfect hitter's stance. Ben nodded, impressed.

"You ready?" Ben asked. Cory nodded. Ben pulled his knee up and his arm back and lobbed a pitch toward Cory.

THWACK!

Cory connected and nailed the ball so hard it flew over Ben's head. The little guys in the outfield scrambled toward it, bumping into each other and bursting out laughing. Jack and Hero ran after the ball, racing each other. Hero got to it first, just before it rolled downhill at the edge of the clearing. Jack wrestled the ball playfully from Hero's mouth. Scout ran over and tried to snatch it back, chasing Jack around the outfield. Jack laughed loud and long.

"Hey, you two!" Ben called out. "He's gonna score! Throw the ball!"

Sure enough, Cory stepped on Ben's backpack, then Jack's, then rounded Ben's hat toward home.

"Get him!" Ben cried. Jack lobbed the ball, and Ben realized they had no catcher. He dashed in from the pitcher's mound, but didn't make it in time. Cory put his foot down on Noah's backpack just as the ball smacked into the ground. Ben was still a few feet away.

"Home run!" Noah cheered, picking Cory up in a bear hug.

Cory raised his arms in the air in triumph, while Noah spun him around and his teammates cheered. Cory looked like a kid without a care in the world. His face was lit up with joy, and he grinned from ear to ear.

For one beautiful, unforgettable moment, the Boy Scouts didn't look cold and wet. They didn't seem to care that it was raining again, or that they'd just barely survived a hurricane. They didn't look scared or exhausted. They just looked like kids playing a pickup game of baseball. And up in the air, his damp hair flying out around him, Cory looked to Ben like any happy kid who'd just hit a home run.

20

THEIR HOOTS AND HOLLERS ECHOED ACROSS the valley
below them. Ben and Jack had an ace slugger on their
team, it turned out—Diego, the tiniest of all the Boy
Scouts, a skinny blond kid with a killer swing. He sent
the ball whizzing past Noah. Hero went after it, and
Noah chased Hero in a circle while the little kids cackled.

The cool air felt gentle and clean on Ben's face. He
looked up at the sky, where he saw a faint glimmer of
light on the horizon. It was dawn—they had been out
in the woods for more than twelve hours. The sun came
up quickly and began to warm them.

The hurricane had passed.

It was Ben's turn at bat. He stepped to Noah's

backpack and tapped the tip of the branch on the ground a couple times. As he raised the wood over his shoulder, something caught his eye—something in the sky beyond the outfield. Ben couldn't believe what he was seeing.

"Look at that." He laughed, pointing. Jack, Noah, and the Boy Scouts spun around and turned their gaze upward. They let out a collective gasp as they saw it too—a crystal clear, perfect rainbow arcing across the sky like a beacon of hope to them all.

And then, in the distance, Ben heard the sound he'd been waiting for since the second he hung up the phone with his dad: helicopters. Their rotors churned in the distance, drawing nearer and growing louder by the second.

"They're here!" the little boys screamed, jumping up and down on the wet ground.

"Quick—make an X!" Emmett yelled out, and the other Boy Scouts immediately knew what he meant. They ran over to him, fell into a single-file line, and began dragging the toes of their right hiking boots through the mud, digging a deep rut in the wet earth. First they dug out a straight line, about ten feet long. Then they made a second line that crossed the first at an angle.

It was a perfect X carved out in the ground, and it would be visible from the sky, a signal for the helicopter. Jack, Noah, and Ben exchanged a look and nodded at each other, impressed.

The sound of the chopper blades got louder. "Okay, kids, let's give the helicopters some space," Jack called out. He and Noah herded the boys toward the back of the clearing, against a large rock. The first helicopter grew larger and larger until it was right above them, while the second one hovered on the opposite side of the clearing. Their hair whipped around, and their hats flew off their heads. Hero ran over to Ben and sat down next to him, leaning against Ben's leg. Scout scuttled over to Jack. Jack picked up the puppy and held him tight.

Ben wondered if they would all fit in one helicopter or if they would have to split up into two groups. At least the Boy Scouts were little. He looked back at them, huddled together with Noah and Jack.

Ben froze. Something wasn't right. In fact, something was terribly wrong.

There were only six Boy Scouts.

He counted again, just to be sure. Six. He looked at their faces—who was missing?

It only took him a second to realize who it was. *Cory.*

Ben's heart pounded in his chest. How long had Cory been gone? How did he let this happen? Ben kicked at the ground in frustration. He fumbled around in his backpack. Sure enough, the walkie-talkie was gone.

Cory had taken it with him. And Ben knew exactly where he had gone: back to his dad. There was no other explanation. Ben understood why—he would never have been able to leave his own dad there, alone and hurting so badly. But still. Didn't Cory realize how dangerous it was out there, especially by himself? Images flashed through Ben's mind: the alligator's snapping jaws, the flash flood filling the valley in seconds, the mud swallowing the creek and raging toward them. He shuddered.

They would never have made it through without each other—Ben, Noah, Jack, Hero, and Scout had all worked together to get them to safety. Cory was so young and small, and the forest was huge. What if he got off the path? What if he got lost trying to get back to his dad? What if he couldn't find the cave, and now father and son were both in danger?

Ben's throat was tight with fear. A rope ladder was unfurling from the closest helicopter, and several men in full uniform and gear were swinging down toward them. The noise was deafening—he knew Jack and Noah wouldn't be able to hear him, even if he could yell right now.

There was no time to wait.

"Hero, let's go!" Ben said. While everyone else kept their eyes locked on the helicopters, Ben and Hero took off running down the trail.

The farther they descended along the path, the darker it got as the trees blocked out the early morning sunlight.

They rounded a curve, and Ben found himself standing in front of a fallen tree blocking his path. Hero dashed under it. Ben had no choice but to do the same. The trunk was unsteady, and Ben held his breath as he ducked under it.

They continued downhill, and Ben wondered how Cory could have gotten so far so fast. He called Cory's name and scanned the tree line for any sign of the boy. Nothing.

Then Ben heard a sound that made his mouth go dry with fear. At first he thought his ears were playing tricks on him, but he heard it again.

"Help!"

It was Cory, crying for help somewhere off to the right, toward the raging creek.

"Hero, go get Cory!" Ben commanded. Hero shot

off through the trees. Hero moved so lightly through the woods that Ben couldn't even hear him going. But he did hear the water in the distance, running faster and louder than before.

"Oh no—" Ben muttered as a horrible realization hit him.

Cory wasn't near the water. He was *in* the water. The muddy, raging, dangerous, debris-filled water.

Hero got to Cory first. The boy was in the creek up to his chin. The water churned so hard that it splashed right onto Cory's face, barely giving him time to catch his breath. Cory was clinging tightly to the roots of a tree on the bank. The fast-moving water was gradually pushing him downstream, and his hands were slipping farther and farther toward the end of the roots. He wouldn't be able to hold on much longer.

Hero ran back and forth along the water's edge, his paws splashing in the current. He started to run into the brisk stream toward Cory, just as Ben ran up behind him.

"Hero, wait!" Ben cried. Hero stopped and waited for Ben's command. "Hang on, Cory!"

"I can't!" Cory yelled.

"You have to. Hold on tight," Ben called. "We're

going to get you—you're going to be fine, okay?"

Ben grabbed a long tree branch from the ground. He hefted it with both hands and swung it out over the water. He angled it toward Cory.

"Hang on," Ben said. "Don't reach for it until I tell you to, okay?"

Cory nodded.

Ben walked forward until the water covered his feet. He slipped on the muddy bottom but kept his balance. He positioned the end of the branch as close to Cory's hands as he could and tucked the wide end of it under his armpit to brace it. Then he steadied himself and planted his feet firmly.

"Okay, Cory—slowly now, take one hand off and put it on the branch."

Nervously, Cory did as he was told. He held on to the roots with one hand, and carefully grabbed on to the branch with the other.

"You got it?" Ben asked. Cory nodded. Ben made sure he still had a good hold on the branch. He steadied himself again. Once Cory let go of the roots in the water, his weight would be fully on the branch, and Ben would have to hold on tight—and keep his balance. Ben took a breath and exhaled slowly. Hero darted from Ben toward

Cory and back. He wanted to help, but Ben had to do this one on his own.

"Okay," Ben said, "when I say one, you let go with the other hand and grab on, okay?" Cory nodded. Ben counted out loud this time. "Three . . . two . . . one—go!"

Cory let go of the roots and latched on to the long branch with both hands. Ben staggered under the weight of the boy and the rushing current. He fought to regain his balance. He gripped the branch tightly and took a big step backward, pulling Cory toward the shore.

"Hold on," Ben called out. He took another step back. Cory moved in closer. Ben strained against Cory's weight. Was he getting heavier? How was it getting harder to pull him in instead of easier?

"I think I'm stuck!" Cory screamed. "Ben—my backpack—it's stuck on something!"

"It's okay—I got you, Cory. Don't worry," Ben called back. He hoped he sounded convincing, because he had no idea what to do next. Cory couldn't take off his backpack. If he let go with either hand, he wouldn't be able to hold on, and the water would carry him away. Ben couldn't hold on much longer either. His arms were starting to shake, and sweat broke out on his brow.

His only choice was to push Cory backward a little and hope the pack loosened itself.

"Okay, Cory—here's what we're going to do," Ben said. "I'm going to slowly push you back out into the water a little—"

"No!" Cory cried, terrified. "Please, no—"

The fear in his voice broke Ben's heart.

"It's okay," Ben soothed him. "It's going to be fine. We can do this—think of everything we've done already! This is nothing, right?"

"Right," Cory said, sounding uncertain.

"Okay, here I go." Ben took one small step forward. Cory moved backward in the water. The powerful current buffeted him around, and Ben felt the branch digging into his side. "Hang on," Ben grunted. He took another step forward. Suddenly the stick grew lighter in Ben's hands. It bounced sharply upward, just as Cory let out a scared cry.

Cory had lost his grip. He was only holding on with one small hand.

Ben saw Cory's other hand waving in the air. "Cory! Grab on with both hands!"

"I can't!" Cory shouted back. The strong current pushed him back and forth, and his body bobbed up and down.

Ben didn't know what to do. He couldn't hang on much longer—and neither could Cory.

Suddenly, Ben flew backward, landing on his back in the mud. The tree branch had snapped, and Cory was rushing downstream, trapped in the powerful flow of water.

Ben didn't stop to think. He threw off his backpack, pushed himself up off the muddy ground, and ran straight toward the water. He jumped in and started swimming frantically, trying to reach the boy. But the current was too strong. It knocked Ben around, tossing and spinning him in the water. Hero barked and ran along the shore, keeping pace.

"Cory!" Ben managed to yell before getting a mouthful of muddy water. He coughed it up.

"Ben! Help me!" Cory called from up ahead. Ben tried to straighten himself out so he could swim to Cory, but he couldn't fight the water. The current swept Ben downstream until he bumped into a rock. He reached out to grab it, but his hands slipped right off of the slick, mossy stone.

Hero ran ahead and took a few steps into the rough, murky water. As Cory moved past, his arms flailing in the air, Hero tried to catch hold of Cory's jacket with his teeth. But the tiny boy was moving too fast.

Hero tried again as Ben flew by. Ben reached out a hand to grab on to Hero's collar, but at the last moment, the current yanked Ben in the other direction.

As he swept by, hurtling downstream on the rough water, Ben's fingertips brushed against Hero's soft fur.

21

BEN STRUGGLED TO KEEP HIS FACE above the water so he could breathe. Cory was only a few feet ahead of him now, almost within reach. Ben felt his leg brush against a large rock. Quickly, he kicked off from the rock, propelling himself forward. It worked—he got close enough to grab the strap of Cory's backpack.

Ben pulled Cory in close and held him with one arm around his chest. The boy was shivering from the cold and the shock.

"I got you," Ben said.

Cory spluttered water. "I need to get to my dad."

"The helicopters came," Ben reassured him, spitting

out water so he could talk. "The rescue team is going to find him."

Cory nodded. His teeth chattered.

Ben was trying hard not to panic. He frantically cast his eyes about for something—anything—he could grab to stop them from continuing downstream. But they were in the middle of the creek and moving so fast that every time he spotted a branch or tree root, they swept past it too quickly.

Where was Hero?

With some effort, Ben twisted his body, kicked with both feet and used his free hand to paddle them in a half circle. Finally, he could see forward instead of backward.

Ben spotted Hero up ahead, running at top speed along the edge of the creek. He stopped to look at something. Ben and Cory were hurtling toward him—they had about thirty yards to go before they caught up to him. Ben couldn't tell exactly what Hero was doing—it looked like he was jumping up and down. No—wait—he was slamming himself into something. Ben squinted and shook the water off his face so he could see clearly.

Hero was throwing himself against a fallen tree. The massive trunk leaned precariously against another tree by the creek bed.

Hero was trying to knock it down.

Because if he could knock it down, it would fall across the creek, right in their path. And Ben and Cory would be able to grab on to it for sure.

Every time Ben thought Hero couldn't possibly impress him more, he was wrong. Hero never seemed to run out of ways to prove how amazing he was.

They were drawing closer. Hero was butting his head against the tree, digging his paws into the mud and pushing as hard as he could. Every muscle in his body was flexed, and his fur stood on end. Ben was scared he was going to hurt himself. But he was also scared that Hero wouldn't be able to get the tree down in time, and then what? Hero was their only hope.

The tree trunk wobbled. Hero pushed at it again with the flat part on the top of his head. The trunk shook and started to move forward, then rolled back into place. Hero pushed again. The roots pulled up from the muddy ground, flinging dirt and rocks all over Hero's coat. He gave one more hard push. With a loud crack, the last of the roots gave way, and everything toppled.

The long tree trunk came down with a splash right into the water. Ben and Cory were so close to it that the water sprayed them.

"Hold on tight, okay, Cory?" Ben said.

"Okay," Cory said, his voice small and scared.

As they rushed by, Ben reached out with his free arm and snagged the tree trunk. He and Cory slammed into it with intense force—pain radiated from Ben's ribs through his entire body. But he didn't care. He squeezed the trunk tightly and helped Cory wrap both arms around it too.

"Go!" Ben said. Cory scrambled arm over arm along the trunk, pulling himself toward the shore. Hero waited for him there. As soon as Cory got close enough, Hero ran into the water, latched on to Cory's jacket with his teeth, and began pulling him onto land. Cory rolled onto the ground, coughing and spitting up water. He turned onto his stomach and got on all fours. Hero sniffed at him and licked the water off his face.

Ben pulled himself toward land. He crawled onto the muddy ground, gasping for air. It was only then, when he was out of the water, that he realized how cold he was. His whole body began to shake uncontrollably—as much from the cold as from the adrenaline that coursed through him.

Hero ran to Ben and licked his face and neck. After a moment, when he could control his limbs again, Ben reached out an arm and wrapped it around his dog's neck. He buried his face in Hero's fur. Ben found his voice.

"Thank you, Hero. You saved us."

22

HERO RAN TO THE TOP OF the hill, ahead of the boys. Ben and Cory were moving slowly, their limbs still warming up. Ben's entire body hurt from head to toe. He started imagining something he hadn't allowed himself to think about since they'd left his house the day before: a hot shower and his own bed.

Ben and Cory climbed to the top of the hill and stepped off the path into the clearing. It was alive with activity. The helicopters still hovered on either side. A dozen rescue crew members were swarming around the Boy Scouts. The kids were wrapped in shiny metallic thermal blankets. Most of them were crying—with relief, Ben knew. More men scrambled down the rope ladder of the second chopper.

"Watch out—coming through!" Ben stepped aside as a group of the burliest men he had ever seen barreled past him, carrying a stretcher. Marco was on it with his eyes closed in pain, his leg strapped down. He winced with every bounce and bump.

"Dad!" Cory yelled as they passed. Marco opened his eyes and smiled at his son, reaching a hand out to him. Cory's face lit up from within.

Ben scanned the crowd. From a distance, he spotted his dad speaking frantically into his cell phone. He held a folded map in the other hand. Ben knew his dad was desperately trying to find him, and a sharp pang of guilt shot through him. Ben felt sick at the thought of what he'd put his dad through.

Ben watched as Hero crossed the clearing in a few long strides and ran to Ben's dad. Hero jumped up on him with his front legs, knocking the map from his hands.

Ben's throat tightened as his dad looked up and saw him. His dad ran across the clearing, scooping Ben up in a massive bear hug.

"I'm so glad you're okay—"

"—Dad, I'm so sorry—"

Ben felt Hero jump on them as they hugged. He stepped back to let Hero join in their embrace, and he and his dad burst out laughing. They looked at each other.

"Ben," his dad said, "I could kill you if I wasn't so happy to see you."

Ben hung his head. "I wouldn't blame you." He didn't know how he could feel so joyous and so awful at the same time. He wished he could have it both ways—he wouldn't change any of what happened if it would save Jack, Scout, and the Boy Scout troop again. But he would never wish this kind of worry and fear on his family, not for a second. He didn't know how to tell his dad that these two feelings took up equal space in his chest.

But he didn't have to. He looked up at his dad.

"Look, Ben," his dad said, his hand on his shoulder and his eyes locked on Ben's. "I know as well as anyone that it takes great risk to save lives. And I know what it feels like to have that—that *drive* in your heart. But I'm just not ready for my son—for you—to be the one taking that risk."

Ben hung his head. "I know, Dad. I know."

"Sergeant Landry," a uniformed man called out, waving him over. "We're ready to load them up."

"Coming," Ben's dad replied. He turned to Ben. "You want to go home?"

"I sure do," Ben said. "Let's get out of here."

"By the way, do I even want to know why you're soaking wet?" Ben's dad asked with a shake of his head.

"Not really." Ben grinned.

Ben and Hero followed Ben's dad to the nearest helicopter. Jack held Scout in one arm and pulled himself up the rope ladder with the other. Noah followed closely behind. One by one, the Boy Scouts made their way up the ladders of the two aircraft—tiny specks clinging to the rungs.

Ben and his father waited for the last of the kids to climb. Ben tipped his head back and followed the ladder with his eyes. It flapped in the stiff breeze of the helicopter's blades. He sucked in his breath. Ben looked back at his dad, who nodded.

"I'll be right behind you," his dad said. "With this guy." He gestured at Hero, who waited patiently by his side. His dad clipped a strong rope to Hero's harness, which the guys in the chopper would use to pull Hero up to safety. Hero could climb ladders—but not one that loose in such a strong wind.

Ben took a deep breath and grabbed hold. He stepped onto a low rung and the ladder swayed under his weight. He pulled himself up and started to climb.

23

THE BRIGHT LIGHTS WERE SHINING RIGHT in Ben's eyes. He couldn't see anyone in the audience, but he could hear his mom and dad, Noah's parents, Jack's mom—and Jack's dad—cheering from the front row. Ben's kid sister Erin's high-pitched voice rose above the crowd. "Goooooo, Benny!" she shouted.

Ben put his hand on Hero's head and scratched him behind the ears. Hero's tail thumped on the ground next to him. Noah stood on one side of Ben, Jack on the other.

"We are starting to run out of ways to recognize the bravery of the Landry family—and now their friends," the mayor said with a chuckle into the microphone at the podium. The crowd went nuts, cheering and clapping. The mayor waited for the noise to die down. "And we are definitely running low on adjectives for their amazing dog, Gulfport's own search-and-rescue hero, Hero."

The hoots and hollers and clapping were so loud that Ben's eardrums tingled. Hero didn't seem to mind. He just looked out at the boisterous crowd with his usual calm expression. He let out a short, sharp bark and wagged his tail some more.

"But hopefully this medal of honor from the city of Gulfport will express our gratitude once again." The mayor was trying to wrap up his speech, but he was having trouble getting through it with all the interruptions. Especially from Ben, Noah, and Jack's teammates, who released a loud, coordinated "*Whoooooooooop!*" every few minutes—followed by a chorus of young Boy Scouts in uniform screaming "*Yaaaaaayyyyyy!*"

Ben's cheeks burned with embarrassment every time the audience let loose. It was hard to resist the temptation to roll his eyes, but he didn't think his mom would appreciate a photo like that ending up in the paper. Instead he tried to remember all the things he planned to say to his very loud friends the second this was over.

Ben was hot in his suit. He didn't love the way the

stiff collar of his dress shirt scratched at his neck. He definitely hated the tie and clunky shoes. But he was proud to be standing onstage, with Hero at his side. He couldn't deny that it felt pretty good to have helped someone—well, lots of people this time.

Over the last couple of weeks, every time he thought about Cory's face the moment he saw that his dad, Marco, was okay . . . Ben didn't know the right words to describe the feeling. He just knew that he wanted to have it again. He knew he wanted to save people for a living.

There would always be danger involved. He got that—and he knew his parents would not be happy about it. But all of Ben's worries and fears were calmed by the knowledge that he had a powerful ally in his corner: Hero.

As long as Ben and Hero were a team, he wasn't afraid.

ACKNOWLEDGMENTS

Huge thanks to Les Morgenstein, Josh Bank, Sara Shandler, and Romy Golan at Alloy; Margaret Anastas, Cheryl Eissing, and the Harper sales, marketing, and publicity teams; and Katelyn Hales at the Robin Straus Agency.

Huge gratitude to Hayley Wagreich and Robin Straus—you are patient, kind, and really good at keeping wandering writers on track.

And huge love to Virginia "Gigi" Wing; Kunsang "Somo" Bhuti; my husband, Brian; and—of course—the goons. You make it all worthwhile (not to mention possible)!

Don't miss these books by
JENNIFER LI SHOTZ!

Get ready for canine adventures full of danger, loyalty, and the heroics of man's best friend.

HARPER
An Imprint of HarperCollinsPublishers

www.harpercollinschildrens.com